Fiona and the Forgotten Piano

by

Kate DeMaio

Wild Ink Publishing LLC

Copyright © 2025 Kate DeMaio

All rights reserved.

No part of this publication may be reproduced, distributed, or transmitted in any form or by any means, including photocopying, recording, or other electronic or mechanical methods, without the prior written permission of the publisher, except as permitted by U.S. copyright law. For permission requests, contact [include publisher/author contact info].

The story, all names, characters, and incidents portrayed in this production are fictitious. No identification with actual persons (living or deceased), places, buildings, and products is intended or should be inferred.

Editor: Laura Wackwitz

Cover Design: Olivia Hunter

Layout Design: Abigail Wild

ISBN: 978-1-958531-81-5

For Grandma

Chapter 1

The sign at the edge of the Fermata woods wasn't big or bright or loud. It was small, wooden, and obscured by ivy vines. It was about the size of a cat who is curled up for an afternoon nap, and it was held in the ground by a stake that looked as sturdy as uncooked spaghetti. Almost no one knew the sign was there.

Fiona knew though. She recognized the little things. The things that were insignificant to others. Maybe she was one of those things.

Though the sign at the edge of the woods was odd, the problem with it wasn't that it was small or unstable. The problem was that even if the occasional passerby did stop to read it, they would learn little more about the woods than someone who hadn't noticed it at all. The sign read:

Fermata Woods

176 acres

Est.

It was puzzling. Normally, when the letters E-S-T are followed by a period at the bottom of a sign, they are meant to be followed by a date. Est. is an abbreviation for the word established, after all. Fiona knew this because her school had a similar message carved into one of the stones at the entrance to the building. The stone said SONGFIELD ELEMENTARY, SONGFIELD, MASSACHUSETTS. EST. 1909. That sign made sense. 1909 was the year the school was built. But the sign at the edge of the woods was different. It had no year after the Est. And it didn't appear as though the year had faded away over time since the rest of the words on the sign were perfectly clear.

Perhaps the missing date was a message. It was as if to say that the exact date at which the woods became the woods didn't matter. It only mattered that they were there at all.

It must've taken a great deal of effort to establish these woods. From the bits and pieces Fiona could see of them, they seemed to hold every kind of tree imaginable. There was a graceful silk tree whose thread-like pink flowers dotted its branches like cotton candy. There was a humble silver birch whose leaves collected delicate snow each winter, as if protecting the fragile flakes from the harsh earth. Fiona could only dream of what trees lay deeper in the woods.

And though Fiona did dream of the woods—quite often in fact—no one else seemed interested in them. She wondered if the little sign was to blame. Or perhaps everyone was just too busy to notice how special the woods were.

On this particular afternoon, as Fiona passed the sign on her walk home, she ran her fingers over its rough edges as a way of saying *I see you*. The sign answered back with a sharp poke to her pointer finger. She winced and held the stinging finger in her hand. A thin splinter lay beneath the top layer of skin. She pushed her thumbnail against the splinter in an attempt to push the pointy bugger out. It didn't budge. Fiona bit her cheek. She would have to pick up the pace now. Her piano lesson was starting soon, and she couldn't practice with a splinter poking into her with every note she played.

Fiona eyed the woods beyond the sign. They were peaceful, shaded from the too-hot-for-fall sun. A light breeze danced through the trees, and the leaves blew a pleasant swishing sound over her ears. Fiona's home was on the other side of the woods. If she was allowed to walk through them, she might be able to shave ten minutes off her walk—not that she'd ever tried.

Her mouth pulled to one side. She considered it, just for a moment. She could break the rules. Other eleven-year-olds broke the rules all the time.

But Fiona's feet remained glued to the sidewalk. She couldn't bring herself to move them any closer to the trees. She wasn't allowed in the woods. And her mom would know if she entered them. Mothers always know. Fiona shifted uncomfortably. She wiggled her toes in her shoes, willing her feet to make a decision. Finally, she turned her focus away from the woods to the path she walked every day. She lengthened her stride and marched around the woods toward home.

♪♫♪♫♪♫

Fiona's mother freed the splinter from her finger just in time for Ms. Downey's arrival. A single stern knock rang in the living room. Ms. Downey was the only person Fiona knew who only knocked once. Most people knocked at least three times. Some knocked with a playful tune. For Ms. Downey, one knock was enough to make her presence known.

Fiona opened the door to see her piano teacher looking as gloomy as usual. She had the constant appearance of someone who had been caught in the rain. Though the weather was perfectly sunny, her hair was flat and heavy. Her makeup was applied in haphazard blotches and in the places where her foundation wasn't thick enough, her skin was pale and drained.

Ms. Downey's clothes held no color. She wore black pointed boots, a long wool skirt, and a cardigan whose sleeves draped inches below her fingertips. Fiona couldn't tell whether it was piano lessons she disliked or whether it was the shadow cast over them by her teacher. But at least Ms. Downey never mentioned Fiona's spots.

Fiona had the feeling her mother felt the same way about Ms. Downey. She always adorned the piano with a bouquet of fresh flowers before Fiona's lesson. Maybe she hoped the color would bring some life to Ms. Downey's gray mood. Today's bouquet was a true ray of sunshine filled with daffodils, tulips, and an overbearing sunflower whose stem struggled to hold its large head up.

Ms. Downey's eyes flicked up at the bouquet for just a moment before she focused her gaze on the piano keys. She took a seat at the bench and, without looking at Fiona, she said flatly, "Scales."

Fiona hurriedly sat down next to Ms. Downey. She straightened her spine and pushed her shoulders back—Ms. Downey hated bad posture. Fiona cleared her throat, hesitant to ask her question. "W-which scales, Ms. Downey?"

"Start with major, then natural minor, and finish with chromatic."

Fiona forced a small smile though her stomach sank. This lesson was going to be as boring as the last. She'd practiced scales practically all summer. Surely she could learn a song by now. But Fiona didn't argue. She rested her fingertips on the keyboard and began to play. Ms. Downey closed her eyes to listen.

By this time, Fiona was so well practiced at scales she hardly had to think of them as she played. Her fingers knew what to do. Her mind was free to wander. But it often clung to places she didn't want to go. It took her to the playground where she first realized she didn't look like everyone else. Where the girl who had finally agreed to play with Fiona was dragged away by her mother who screamed—*Thunk.*

Thunk. Thunk.

Fiona was pulled back into her lesson. She pressed her finger down on a black key. It shifted only slightly before sticking in place. Ms. Downey's eyes narrowed. "Your mother has been leaving the windows open again. How many times do I have to tell her? Humidity will make the keys stick."

Fiona said nothing. She couldn't agree with Ms. Downey without telling on her mother, but she couldn't disagree without lying to her teacher.

Ms. Downey fiddled with the sticking key. "Do you know what note this is supposed to be?"

"It's a C sharp," Fiona replied with all the confidence she had.

Ms. Downey pressed her lips together. Fiona's confidence began to slip away. But she couldn't be wrong, keys and notes were practically the only thing she knew about music.

After another moment, Ms. Downey seemed to decide the silence had gone on long enough. "Keys can be more than one note. You should know that. It's the same way you refer to your mother as 'mom' but I call her 'Victoria.' This key is both a C sharp and a D flat. I suppose we'll keep working on scales until you've learned that."

Once again, Fiona pasted a small smile across her face. It was perhaps less convincing than the first grin. But she was sure Ms. Downey didn't notice. Patience was one of Fiona's stronger qualities.

"Right, well. I suppose I'll have to have a talk with your mother. Where is she do you think? In the kitchen?"

Fiona nodded and Ms. Downey left the room. Maybe if the key were fixed by the time Ms. Downey returned, her teacher's mood would improve. Maybe Fiona could even ask to learn a song. It wouldn't have to be anything fancy. She would be happy just learning "Twinkle Twinkle Little Star."

Fiona set about fixing the key. She pushed her thumb against the corner of the black key and tried to lift it up. She tapped the white keys surrounding it a few times. Then she pressed her foot on a pedal at the base of the piano and tried lifting the black key again. It stuck. She folded her hands in her lap and sighed.

But then she heard it.

She heard the note the key was supposed to play. It was clear and loud and crisp. Only the note wasn't coming from the piano. It couldn't be. She hadn't pressed the key again. The note lingered, filling the room with its soft hum. Fiona glanced around to see where it was coming from. There were no other instruments nearby. There were no speakers. No computers. No televisions. No one else was in the room with her.

The note stopped abruptly.

Fiona stood. She didn't know why exactly she stood, but the piano was freaking her out a bit. She felt like giving the instrument its space.

Then all at once the sound came again. A different note this time—a C from the great octave. This time, Fiona searched the room. She lifted the couch cushions. She pulled books off the shelves. She lifted the rug. Surely someone was playing a prank on her. But who and why?

Fiona opened the window, and the note enveloped her. It had the sensation of diving underwater. The sound was warm and heavy. It drowned everything else out. It was as though the note was pulling her beneath the surface of this world and into another one. But where was the sound coming from? Fiona scanned her empty yard. She searched the shadows in the woods. She wasn't looking for anything in particular. She didn't know what could be making the sound. She might know it if she saw it. She looked for anything out of the ordinary. But there was only the woods.

Was it possible…?

No. It couldn't be.

But maybe…

Maybe the sound was coming from the trees themselves.

The note stopped just as Ms. Downey returned to the living room. Fiona's head was still halfway out the window. "So, it's you I should blame for leaving the windows open." Fiona quickly pulled her head inside and slid the window shut. "Quite rude of you to let me reprimand your mother for it. You should have taken responsibility when I mentioned the windows the first time."

Fiona's lips parted, but she had no reply.

"Anyway, I overheard you got that key to work but we are out of time for today. I'll see you at the recital."

The recital.

An uneasy feeling crept its way up Fiona's stomach and into her throat. She swallowed. Was the recital tomorrow already? Ms. Downey hadn't told her what she should play. There was nothing she could play. Were there songs that could be made using just scales?

Ms. Downey picked her purse off the floor and made her way to the front door, tripping on the overturned rug as she left.

Chapter 2

Fiona sat in an uncomfortable wooden chair in the back row of the hall. The stage at the front of the room was raised only slightly above the rest of the floor, but it seemed to tower over the audience. To say Fiona had butterflies was an understatement. It felt more like a swarm of bees was trying to escape her stomach. She straightened her pleated skirt against her lap and tucked in her blouse for the fourth time.

Fiona's mother reached over to grab her hand and gave it a light squeeze. She whispered in Fiona's ear, "After this we'll go straight home and make Chinese food omelets."

Fiona nodded. Saturday mornings were supposed to be fun. On Saturdays, Fiona and her mother made breakfast out of Friday night's leftovers. Today, it would have to be lunch. The recital was getting in the way of their tradition.

Fiona glanced at the clock, but she was too nervous to make out what time the hands were pointing to. Hopefully the recital would be over soon. There couldn't be more than a few students left to go. Most of the well-dressed children had already made their way to the stage.

Ms. Downey shuffled to the microphone at the center of the stage. Though it was nearing the end of the recital, she still didn't seem to have a handle on how close her mouth should be to the microphone. This time it was too close. She mumbled a name Fiona couldn't make out.

A chair squeaked as a young blonde boy stood and approached the stage. He wore an orange tie which must have belonged to his father. It stretched from the boy's neck down to his knees.

The boy took his seat at the piano and began to play something Fiona thought she recognized as Minuet in D Minor. A few of the notes were out of tune. Well, more than a few. Actually, the song sounded a bit like Minuet in Demonic Pigeons but at least the boy had something to showcase. Fiona picked at her nails. Why had Ms. Downey taught this boy a song? He had to be at least a few years younger than she was. And he wasn't very good. Didn't Fiona deserve to learn one too?

"You'll be great no matter what you play," her mother said. "I'm rooting for you."

Fiona smiled sheepishly. She wasn't so sure.

The boy's song finished. He bowed, letting the tip of his tie brush against the floor. A blonde couple, who Fiona presumed to be the boy's parents, stood, and whooped with the enthusiasm of someone who had just seen a cat walking on stilts.

Ms. Downey barely bothered to pick her feet up off the floor as she took to the stage again. Fiona's heartbeat quickened. Her turn would be coming soon. Maybe her teacher would forget about her sitting all the way in the back of the room. It's not like she had anything to perform anyway.

Just as the thought left her brain, Ms. Downey leaned into the microphone and announced, "Fiona Duet is next."

Fiona swallowed. She kept her head down as she made her way to the imposing stage. With every step she took, her palms grew more and more clammy. She wiped them against her skirt.

The piano was grander than the one she had at home. Its sleek black shine was intimidating. Its bench was stiff and unworn. She rested her fingertips on its keys. They were wider than she was used to. She had to spread her fingers a bit further than usual to place them in the right position.

Shoulders back, she could almost hear Ms. Downey thinking from across the room. Fiona straightened her spine.

From somewhere in the audience came a whisper. "What are those things?" the voice said.

There was a giggle in response. No doubt they were noticing her for the first time. Not her exactly, but her spots. The bright red blemishes she had been stuck with since birth. Her skin looked like a canvas for scarlet splatter paint. The doctors said the spots would go away with age, but Fiona was disappointed every morning when she looked in the mirror and saw they were still there.

Sometimes people stared at the spots. Sometimes they pitied her. Fiona had grown used to the stomach-twisting feeling she got when people reacted that way. But sometimes... sometimes her spots scared people. She could recognize it. The moment their faces turned from confusion to fear. They thought she had an incurable disease she would pass on to them if they came within an arm's distance of her. She couldn't leave the house without at least one of those looks. Why should today be any different?

Fiona's chest tightened. She closed her eyes and tried to ignore the crowd. She let her fingers play the scales she knew so well.

Only it wasn't scales her fingers chose to play. It was a perfect rendition of Minuet in D Minor. The boy's performance swam through her mind. It ran down her arms and into her fingertips. Except, when Fiona played it, there were no mistakes. She didn't know how she was doing it. Her eyes flickered open. She managed a glance at Ms. Downey. Was this part of the plan? Was memorizing scales some secret method to learning how to play real music?

Ms. Downey's stare barreled into her like bowling balls. So, this wasn't supposed to happen then. She wasn't supposed to know how to play anything other than scales.

Yet, her fingers continued.

The song finished.

Fiona had finished it. Though it didn't quite feel like she had played it. It felt like a secret door in the back of her mind had been unlocked. It creaked open just enough to let one song out.

Fiona stood a little shakily and turned to the audience. She caught a glimpse of the boy with the long tie. He looked as angry as Ms. Downey had. His father crossed his arms and shook his head. "Where does she get the nerve?" the boy's mother said, her words echoing in the hall.

The audience clapped uncomfortably, and Fiona deflated. She didn't like upsetting people. She hadn't meant to play better than the boy. It had just... happened. She looked to Ms. Downey for some sort of explanation. Her teacher was clearly upset but maybe she could at least diffuse the tension in the room. But Ms. Downey's chair was empty. Fiona scanned the hall. Her teacher was nowhere to be seen.

Fiona bit her lip and returned to her seat without a bow.

A greasy paper bag sat on the kitchen table. The name V. Duet was written across it in thick black marker. Fiona's mother poured a beaten-egg mixture into a warm cast iron pan. Today's omelet would be filled with sesame chicken, broccoli, and bell pepper. Fiona was excited to try this one, especially because last weekend they'd had fried fish omelets, and no amount of ketchup could make those taste good.

Fiona's mother mumbled to herself as she cooked the eggs. "Tent... spent... vent." She did that sometimes, muttered rhymes to herself. It was her way of passing the time, Fiona thought.

Fiona joined in. "Invent, accent, cement," she said, grabbing a plate from the cabinet. She carried the plate to the table feeling lighter than she had all morning. The nerves of the recital flaked off her like breadcrumbs.

Fiona positioned herself in her favorite chair. The one that allowed her to see the woods through her back door. The mysterious sound she'd heard the day before was weighing on her mind. Last night, she'd dreamt she was running barefoot over the cool, damp dirt of the forest floor. Music swam around her like a school of fish. The notes caught sunlight and sparkled as they bounded from one tree to the next. It was only a dream, but it was so vivid it felt almost like a memory. Now she found it hard to keep her eyes off the woods. Would they sing to her again today?

Maybe the leftover fortune cookie would tell her. Fiona leaned forward and grabbed the paper bag. One lonely fortune cookie sat at the bottom of it. She looked hopefully at her mother.

"Go ahead," her mother intoned.

Fiona grinned and pulled the cookie from the bag. She struggled a bit with the plastic wrapper, but when she finally cracked it open, she read the fortune aloud.

> You already have all that you need.
> Lucky numbers: 16, 41, 57.

Her mother cocked her head, considering the fortune. "Not very original, but true enough."

"I think it means you don't have to add hot sauce to the omelet," Fiona said.

"Oh, does it?" her mother asked, a smile evident in her voice as she fumbled through the spice cabinet. "You're right. Soy sauce would be more fitting."

Fiona shook her head.

"Quite an impressive performance today," Fiona's mother said as she scooped a fluffy omelet onto Fiona's plate.

Fiona blushed. She had been too distracted by the reactions of the rest of the crowd to notice what her mother had thought of her recital. "I, um…" Fiona shrugged as she trailed off. She couldn't explain what had happened. She quietly ate her omelet to fill the space hovering between her and her mom.

Her mother nodded as if Fiona had finished her sentence. "After lunch, would you mind cutting some fresh flowers from your father's garden? The bouquet over the piano is looking a bit wilted."

"Sure. No problem." Fiona said, happy to change the subject.

A cloud passed over the sun causing the light outside to dim. Something caught Fiona's eye out the window. A stroke of black floated between the trees.

"Did you..." Fiona trailed off as she tracked the shadowy figure. It swept along the tree line. It was human-shaped. But something wasn't right about it. As it moved, it seemed to leave a bit of itself behind, like a smudge. "Did you invite anyone over, Mom?"

"Hmm?" her mother replied, her mouth quite full of omelet.

Fiona moved to the window. "There's someone..."

Suddenly, Fiona's mother was at the window blocking her view. "It's rude to leave the table without being excused." Her tone was more serious than usual. It caught Fiona off guard. Even stranger, her mother had never mentioned this rule before. Fiona always followed the rules. She wouldn't have left the table if she had known she had to ask first. It seemed the older Fiona got, the more rules were added to the list. It was becoming difficult to keep track of them all.

"Sorry, I didn't know. It's just—" Fiona lifted her finger to point out the window, but her mother's face told her to drop it.

"Have a seat, Fee. I hope I didn't spoil your lunch with that fortune cookie."

"You didn't," Fiona said. She sat back in her seat and tried her very best to ignore the woods.

Chapter 3

Flimsy floral shoots brushed against Fiona's calves as she tiptoed through her father's garden. She knelt among the lilies and cut them one by one at the base of their stems. She faced the woods, still unsure about what she'd seen earlier. Had she imagined the dark figure running through the trees? Was it a deer? Or maybe a lost dog? Those things seemed more likely. She shook her head to clear the shadowy image from her mind.

When Fiona had a sizable collection of lilies, a tingling sensation crawled over her toes. She had pins and needles from sitting on them too long. She shifted her weight to her other foot, and her knee collided with something hard and sharp. She gasped, not expecting the pain. Fiona rolled to her side, crushing a few asters as she did. She raised her knee to look at it and brushed off the dirt that stuck to her skin. There was a small indent where the object had pushed into her kneecap, but there was no blood. What had she knelt on?

Fiona patted her hand along the dirt until she felt a spot where the soil didn't compact as much as she pressed on it. She dug her fingers into the ground. Granules of cool dirt slid under her nails. She closed her hand over an object. She had planned to toss it straight across the yard so she wouldn't accidentally sit on it again, but somewhere in the clump of dirt, something glittered. She opened her palm and brushed away the loose soil revealing a rectangular object. It was a little longer than her finger. She rubbed her finger and thumb around each side of the object to clear away more of the dirt. It was some kind of block, similar to the kind used to play Jenga. Only it looked like this block was decades old. Perhaps sitting in the ground had aged it.

Three sides of the block were wooden. The fourth was covered in a shimmering white reflective material. It picked up the orange of the lilies and the blue of the sky as she rotated it. Fiona didn't know much about gardening. Maybe the little block was used for something, like steadying weak roots. She carried it to an empty flowerpot and dropped it inside. She would tell her dad about it when he got home. Fiona gathered up the cut lilies and headed towards the back door.

Then a branch snapped behind her.

She froze. The pain in her knee had distracted her. She'd forgotten about the shadow. She had forgotten to face the woods. Her back was towards them now. She stiffened and turned around slowly.

There was nothing.

Nothing out of the ordinary anyway. Only grass and trees and woods. Though the sun was starting to dip below the treeline. If there was a shadow in the woods, it would be harder to make out now.

Fiona peered through her back door window. The kitchen was empty. Her mother was probably in her office. She wouldn't notice if Fiona got just a little closer to the woods. Fiona shuffled forward, inching her way towards the authoritative pine tree at the edge of her yard. It was the place where the woods both began and ended. Fiona would only get in trouble if she entered the woods so surely the pine tree was fair game.

A pop of color bounced in the peripherals of Fiona's vision. Her mouth pulled to one side. Shadows aren't colorful. Whatever was moving, whatever had caused the branch to snap had to be something else. It might've been the soccer ball she'd kicked into the woods over the summer. Maybe a squirrel had gotten a hold of it. She had liked the bright orange ball. She liked how it stood out among the black and white ones.

Fiona wrapped an arm around the towering pine tree and leaned forward, trying to get a better look at the colorful thing. It didn't change her view much, but it was the best she could do under the circumstances. She was already pushing her mother's boundaries just being near the tree at all.

Suddenly, the ball jumped.

It jumped again.

The ball was getting closer. It was unusual behavior. Maybe the squirrels were having an entire scrimmage. But although the ball was jumping in her direction, it didn't grow in size the way objects usually do the closer you get to them. Fiona cocked her head. These woods were growing stranger each day, each hour even. Now they were defying the laws of physics. Maybe this should have made Fiona nervous, but she was buzzing. It hadn't been just her imagination all these years. The woods were special.

The orange dot was only an arm's length away when Fiona finally saw the beady black eyes on the little orange body.

The ball wasn't a ball.

It was a frog.

The frog had apricot skin and blueberry legs. He was covered in black iridescent spots, not unlike Fiona's red ones. The frog was alone too, like Fiona sometimes felt. She bent to meet the frog's gaze. Slowly and deliberately, she reached out her hand, ignoring the voice in her head that warned the frog could be poisonous. The small creature was unusual. Fiona had only ever seen green and brown frogs by her house. This frog had either escaped captivity, or he was very far from home. And something in Fiona, something deep down in her gut, told her she could become his home.

"It's alright," she said, urging the frog closer. "I bet the woods are cold. I can find a warm spot for you in my room."

The frog blinked.

Fiona tried again. "And I'll catch lots of flies for you. Juicy flies and fat mosquitos and"—she nearly gagged—"and thick squirmy worms."

The frog leapt into Fiona's outstretched hand. His little feet were smooth and moist against her palm, which he fit in perfectly. Fiona held her hand as steady as she could as she carried the frog back to her house. When she reached the back door, the frog crouched. It seemed he was already changing his mind about her. He was going to pounce. Fiona quickly put her other hand over the frog's body and twisted the door open with her forearms. She had to find a place to put the frog where he wouldn't jump away. She moved to the kitchen counter and opened her palms just enough so the frog's feet could touch the cold granite surface. Leaving her hands over his body like a cocoon, she made a plan. She needed a pot or a jar. She needed some kind of container she could hold him in for a while.

Fiona scooted her lower half towards the refrigerator. She wrapped her foot around the door handle and pulled it open. The refrigerator door held the usual suspects. Milk, ketchup, mayonnaise, mustard. And pickles. There were only a few left. Though she couldn't grab the pickle jar without taking her hands off the frog. The refrigerator door swung shut.

Fiona slid open her palms just enough to look into the frog's eyes. His little body trembled. "If you could just hang on one second," she said. "I just need a place to put you before I can get those bugs I promised."

Fiona paused, waiting for a sign from the frog that he would stay put. When none came, she had to risk it. Slowly she lifted her hands away from the amphibian. His eyes shifted from one side of the room to the other, but he remained in his spot on the counter. Fiona opened the fridge again, this time with her hand, and pulled out the mostly empty pickle jar. She stuffed the last two salty sour pickles into her mouth. Pickle juice dripped onto her shirt. She chewed as quickly as she could. She tossed the rest of the juice down the sink and plopped the frog into the jar.

The frog's eyes watered with alarm as he blinked in the vinegar smell from the jar's recent occupants. "Sorry," Fiona whispered. "I know that was kind of scary. But please don't worry. I'll keep you safe."

The frog frowned. He didn't seem convinced.

Fiona lifted the pickle jar, making sure to move at a pace that wouldn't make the frog more nervous than he already was. She couldn't help but smile at his spots. They reflected everything around him, from the stainless-steel oven to the kitchen chandelier. "I'll call you Ferris," Fiona said, "because you're bright like the lights on a Ferris wheel. Is that okay with you?"

The frog's eyes softened as he met her gaze and Fiona could swear that he nodded.

Fiona was nervous to show Ferris to her mom. If he'd escaped from the zoo, her mother would make her return him. But Fiona couldn't keep Ferris a secret because she needed a ride to the pet store. She moved down the hallway and stood in the doorway to her mother's office. She held the pickle jar behind her back and cleared her throat. "I didn't go into the woods," she began.

Fiona's mom stopped scrolling on her computer. "I didn't think you did. I've warned you about ticks enough for you to know better." She spun around in her chair and raised an eyebrow. "But now you have me a little suspicious."

"I didn't. But while I was outside, I found something. It came out of the woods."

Fiona's mother crossed her arms, waiting for an explanation.

The words rushed out of Fiona's mouth. "I found a frog. He's beautiful. He has spots just like me. I named him Ferris. I was hoping I could keep him."

Her mother tapped her fingers against her crossed arms. Fiona held her breath.

"Let's see him then," she finally said.

Fiona placed the pickle jar on the desk.

Her mother leaned forward in her chair, meeting the frog at eye level. "Lovely to meet you, Ferris. Let's get you out of this jar."

Chapter 4

For what must've been the fourth time, Fiona picked up Ferris's brand-new hidey hut and moved it to the other side of the tank. The frog begrudgingly followed it. Fiona could tell he wanted to sleep. Each time he crossed his tank, he walked just a bit slower. But she had to make sure everything was in exactly the right place and decisions took time to make.

When Fiona finally turned away from the light of Ferris's heat lamp, she blinked, adjusting her eyes to the darkness that surrounded her. Maybe the frog was right. It was time for bed. Fiona pulled open her dresser and changed into her black and white striped pajamas. Their cuffs hugged her wrist and ankles softly. She tucked herself under the covers of her twin bed where the sheets were cool against her bare feet. Finally, she closed her eyes and lay perfectly still.

Then she turned over.

She took long deep breaths and pushed her nagging thoughts aside to clear her head.

She turned over again.

She couldn't sleep. Something felt wrong, but she wasn't quite sure what it was.

Maybe she needed a change of scenery. She moved her pillow to the other end of the bed and flipped herself around. Still, her eyes would not stay closed. She pressed her eyelids shut, but they popped right back open. Fiona lay awake staring at the ceiling so long the glow-in-the-dark stars stuck up there faded to black.

It was too... quiet. Yes, that was it. Fiona normally fell asleep to the sound of leaves rustling outside her window. She sat up and looked outside. She pushed open her window just a bit. A cool breeze blew into her room. It was too dark to see whether the leaves were dancing in the trees, but it didn't really matter whether she could see them, they had never been this quiet.

And where were the crickets? Their chirping was her lullaby. Sure, the weather had been colder, but it wasn't so cold that the bugs should be hibernating already.

Fiona turned away from the window. She settled back down and rolled onto her side. The strangely quiet woods would have to wait until morning. For now, she had to sleep. Maybe Ferris's croaking could replace the crickets' song.

But Ferris was quiet too. He was climbing the wall of his tank. It was entertaining to watch actually. He moved one sticky foot in front of the other until he was right at the top of it. It was only when Ferris lifted his hand to push on the tank's cover that Fiona realized he was trying to escape. She threw her blankets off and rushed to close the tank securely. She held down the tank's cover. "Excuse me, Mr. Ferris. You're not supposed to leave your tank."

The frog furrowed his brow. Then he spoke. "And why not?" His voice was gravelly, like rolling luggage over pavement.

Fiona paused. If Ferris was speaking, maybe she had fallen asleep. She looked about the room, waiting for the appearance of a hula-hooping elephant or a tutu-wearing dragon, something that would say for sure she was dreaming. When nothing appeared out of the ordinary, she looked at Ferris again and rubbed her eyes. "You're"—she swallowed—"You can talk?"

Ferris rolled his eyes. "Don't act like you haven't heard of talking frogs before. I see *The Frog Princess* right there on your bookshelf." He pointed.

"Books are different from real life," Fiona countered. "You have some explaining to do."

Ferris's eyes widened in disgust. "Oh, *I* have some explaining to do? That's rich coming from the girl who kidnapped me."

"*Kidnapped?*" Fiona took a step back from the tank in surprise.

"I wasn't exactly asking to be captured when you found me," Ferris said.

"You jumped right in my hand!"

"After you bribed me." Ferris growled.

Fiona opened her mouth to speak but she couldn't find the words. She had sort of bribed him, hadn't she? And then she'd stuffed him in a barely clean pickle jar. And she had done it to make herself feel better. "I just... wanted a friend," was all she could say.

Ferris pursed his lips, seeming to understand the sentiment. "Yes, well, no matter the reason, it's time for me to go home."

"So you are from the zoo?" Fiona perked up, curiosity getting the best of her. The closest zoo was a thirty-minute drive away. How could a frog travel that far by himself?

"No, girl." He sighed. "I'm not from the zoo."

"It's Fiona," she corrected.

"What's Fiona?" Ferris asked.

"I am. It's my name."

"Oh." The frog nodded.

A moment of silence passed between them. Fiona shifted the lid on the tank open. Now that she knew Ferris could talk, it was only right to allow him some freedom.

"Where are you from then?" she asked.

"I'm from Fugue." Ferris answered as though it were obvious.

"Fugue," Fiona said, letting the word hang on her lips. She was sure she hadn't heard of it before. "Where is that?"

"Not far, I hope," said Ferris.

"You don't know?" Fiona asked. "How did you get here then?"

Ferris frowned. It seemed like he was trying to remember that himself. "The thing about Fugue, it's... foggy. Very foggy. So foggy you can't see where you're going without a headlamp." Ferris hopped to the top edge of the tank. "I repair headlamps for a living actually," he said, pushing his shoulders back. "The day I got lost was a slow day at the repair shop. I let a customer borrow my headlamp while I repaired theirs. I thought I could fix it quickly and return it that day. But the repair was more difficult than I thought. I needed to keep the broken headlamp overnight, and I had to find my way home blind.

"I know the way. Three jumps southwest. Turn left at the fallen tree. Six jumps forward. Bear right at the waterlilies. Two more jumps then I'm home." Ferris bounced right and left on the tank, reenacting his commute. "But without my headlamp, I was cautious. I wasn't jumping my usual distance. When I got to the waterlilies, I took two leaps forward and landed in complete darkness." Ferris looked down, seeming disappointed in himself. He hopped off the tank down to the table it sat on. Fiona relaxed onto her knees to listen to the story. First, the frog could talk, and now he had a career in a repair shop. It was a lot to take in.

Ferris continued. "The nighttime fog has a bit of a shine to it. But this was different. I couldn't see my own hands on the ground in front of me. I crawled forward and the darkness cleared, but the fog was gone too. The forest was colder than I was used to. And somehow, for the first time in my life, I could see perfectly clearly without a headlamp. I could see the tops of the trees! I knew I was far from home, but I thought I could look around. I wanted to see the blue sky I'd heard about in stories."

Ferris jumped to the floor. "But the woods are big for a frog. I can't tell whether I've seen them all or if I've been walking in circles. I'm not sure how long I've been away from home, if I'm honest." Ferris cast his glance towards the bedroom window. It was still open. "Anyway, I finally made my way to the edge of the woods, and when I saw the sky, I couldn't take my eyes off it. You—well you know what you did. Stuck me in a pickle jar of all things! So, if you don't mind, I'll be on my way."

Suddenly, Ferris leapt three feet in the air onto Fiona's bed. Fiona sprang off her knees, but she wasn't quick enough. With another jump, Ferris leapt out the window.

Fiona's eyes bulged. Her mouth dropped open. Could a frog survive a jump out of a second story window? She didn't have time to think about it. Acting on instinct, Fiona ran out of her room and down the stairs. She wrapped her coat around her shoulders, slipped her feet into sneakers, and placed her hand around the doorknob—all before she thought about what her mother would say.

There was no way she would let Fiona out alone at night.

Heart racing, Fiona glanced up the stairs where she could see the doorway to her parents' room. Their light was still off. She must've been quiet enough as she ran down the stairs that she didn't wake them. Fiona bit her lip. She didn't have time to wake her parents and explain that her talking frog had jumped out the window. He was probably writhing in pain on the ground. He probably had two or three broken legs. She was going to have to perform froggy CPR.

I'll compromise, Fiona thought. Her toes wriggled anxiously in her shoes. *If I ask permission and they don't hear me, at least I asked, right?*

Fiona whispered up the stairs, "Mom, Dad, Ferris jumped out the window. I need to help him. I'll be right back."

Fiona's parents didn't answer, which was expected since they were asleep. So, they hadn't given Fiona permission to leave the house, but they certainly hadn't said no either. Fiona opened the door to the dark, silent yard and immediately turned back around to grab a flashlight.

Chapter 5

Fiona's teeth chattered, whether from the bitter night air or from the nerves pulsing through her, she didn't know. She wished the woods weren't so quiet tonight. Even her ears seemed to notice something was off. There was pressure building inside them, almost as if the air had grown thinner. Her ears didn't seem to know how to behave in the absence of sound. But she could only focus on one strange thing at a time. And right now, a talking frog needed her.

"Ferris," she said in a tone that was simultaneously a whisper and a shout. "Ferris, are you okay?"

The flashlight Fiona found in the kitchen junk drawer was smaller than she had wanted, but when she clicked it on, it was surprisingly powerful. Fiona moved the bright beam of light across the yard desperately hoping for a familiar orange spot to appear.

"Ferris," she called again, raising her voice, too aware of what the neighbors might think if they heard her out this late. *The girl with the spots has finally gone mad.* "Ferris, where are you?" Fiona checked the area below her bedroom window. She dared to take a few steps closer to the woods. She had been at their treeline earlier, but that was when it was light out and when they weren't so eerily silent. "Ferris, if you can move, come here!"

"I'm not a dog," Ferris replied, hovering backside first over an empty flowerpot. His hands were wrapped around the block Fiona had found in the garden earlier.

Fiona dashed to the flowerpot and stooped to Ferris's height. "You're okay. Are you okay? You seem okay. Why did you jump out the window? Why do you have that block?"

Ferris shook his head. "Which of those questions do you want me to answer?"

"The first one." Fiona decided.

"I'm okay," Ferris said, struggling to haul the block out of the pot.

"Oh, thank goodness," Fiona slowly tipped the flowerpot to the ground to prevent Ferris from falling again. "So why did you jump?"

Ferris looked up in earnest. "I have someone waiting for me, Fiona. A family. I can't stay here." He scooted backwards across the back step, keeping his grip on the block.

Fiona's heart sank. Of course, he had a family. He wasn't an escaped zoo animal. He had a home. He had a life before she'd found him. Fiona turned towards the woods. She couldn't keep Ferris, but she could right her wrongs. She could make sure he got home safe. "Listen," she said, glancing towards the trees. She willed them to make a sound, any sound at all. "It's creepy out here. I can walk you home. So you're not alone, I mean."

"It is strange," Ferris agreed, rubbing the place Fiona imagined his ears would be. "Like someone put a blanket over the woods."

"You noticed it too?"

Ferris nodded, and his confidence seemed to falter.

Seeing the crack in Ferris's armor, Fiona seized her opportunity. "It looks like you need help carrying that thing anyway." She gestured to the block. Ferris hadn't loosened his grip on it since she found him.

Ferris looked down at the object, still seeming unable to part with it. "It's important," he said.

"I won't lose it," Fiona promised. "Look, I'm wearing my special jacket. There are four pockets in this thing. And this one"—she tapped the pocket on her upper left, the one by her heart—"this one is for things I care about. Nothing gets lost in here."

Fiona didn't mention the other reason she liked the jacket. Its bright red color distracted from her spots.

"Did you just make that up right now?" Ferris asked, attempting to raise an eyebrow he didn't have.

"Uh-uh," Fiona intoned, placing her hands in the lower two pockets. She pushed her left hand against the coat's fabric forcing it forward. "This pocket is for bulky things that are hard to lose." She pushed her right fist forward. "And this one is for quick access. See how fast I can get in here?" Fiona speedily moved her hand in and out of the pocket.

Ferris chuckled.

"And this top one..." She pressed her hand to her upper right pocket. It made a crinkling sound. She pulled the pocket open and pushed her chin to her neck to peek inside. "I guess I left a snack in here."

Ferris licked his lips at the word snack. Then he shook his head, seeming to clear the thought of food from his mind. "Fine. If that pocket is as safe as you say it is, you can come with me."

♪♪♪♪♪

"20 jumps forward!" Ferris exclaimed, pointing into the darkness. He sat comfortably on Fiona's shoulder, like he belonged there.

Fiona frowned. "Do you really want me to jump?"

"No, I suppose not. How big is one of your steps?"

Fiona took a step forward. "Maybe two feet."

"Whose feet? Mine or yours?"

"No, it's a measurement. There are twelve inches in a foot and three feet make a yard."

Ferris surveyed the backyard. "You can cross this thing in less than two steps?"

"*This* yard isn't three feet. Yards are three feet."

Ferris looked at Fiona through squinted eyes.

She waited for his response, but when none came she said, "Why don't you hop down beside me. You take one jump forward. I'll take one step forward, and we'll see where we end up."

Ferris mumbled something about a "foolish measurement" as he jumped off Fiona's shoulder. He aligned himself with her right shoe and jumped forward.

Fiona took a step forward and saw that Ferris was ahead of her by less than a foot. She took one more step and Ferris was about a foot behind her. "Let's say one and a half steps equals a jump," she suggested.

Ferris grunted. "Okay… hear me out. What if you took bigger steps?"

Fiona considered. If she pointed the flashlight at her feet. She might be able to take bigger steps without tripping. "Let's try it," she agreed.

Ferris rejoined Fiona on her shoulder and declared, "Twenty big steps forward!"

With the flashlight trained on the ground, Fiona took twenty big, purposeful steps. She now stood at the pine tree at the edge of the woods. This was the closest she had come to breaking the rules. It was only this afternoon that she'd dared to even come this far. And now she was going to enter the woods. She had to. For Ferris.

Still, her mother's face appeared in her mind's eye, a look of anger and disappointment plastered onto it. Fiona was going to enter the woods in the silent pitch-black middle of the night and break the rules. She gave the pine tree a pat, hoping it would let her borrow some of its strength.

Ferris tapped his toes excitedly. "Now two steps forward, then eleven steps northwest." He paused to point.

"Northwest is that way in case you have a ludicrous system for direction too."

"No, we have a northwest," Fiona said as she took her first step into the woods.

Fiona swatted at the mosquito that buzzed by her ear. Crickets chirped at her feet. Leaves rustled above her. The woods weren't so quiet now that Fiona was in them. "Ferris, do you feel like we're under the blanket now? The one over the woods?"

Ferris nodded. "It feels like home."

A small smile broke across Fiona's face. She felt lighter, knowing they were close to Fugue. "What's your home like?" she asked.

Ferris didn't say anything at first. It had been an accident he'd left home. Maybe he never had to describe it before. "It's an endless chatter of insects and amphibians. We live around—" He scratched his head. "How do I say this in English? Big Pond, I suppose. We live around Big Pond on brightly painted rocks. The paint helps us find them in the fog. My husband Louis paints them. It's kind of what brought us together. Me with my headlamps and him with his painting, we both help people find their way home."

Fiona swallowed. Even now, when she was supposed to walk Ferris home, he was the one guiding her. He was the perfect guide too. He was cautious yet confident in his directions. He made sure Fiona avoided divots, branches, and fallen trees.

"Are there people in Fugue?"

"Not one," Ferris said, a little too joyfully for her liking.

So Fugue was secluded. At least there wouldn't be anyone there to judge her spots.

"And what is so important about this block?" Fiona tapped the pocket holding the wooden object.

"It's a theory I have," Ferris explained, though it didn't clear anything up.

"A theory about what?" Fiona prompted.

"Left ten steps. The trees here have unusual markings, letters of the alphabet scattered on their trunks. When I was lost, I found a tree marked with the letter A. Then another with an F, one with an AB. I thought it was a catalog of sorts, a way to mark the trees for hikers. But then I stumbled upon this..."

Fiona and Ferris had reached a clearing in the woods. Moonlight crept into Fiona's eyes. She could see better with the break in the tree canopy.

In the center of the clearing stood a sprawling oak tree. Its thick, crooked branches reached out in all directions, like it was trying to connect itself to the other trees. The oak was wide as Fiona was tall. Entwined at the base of the tree was a piano.

"I believe the piano in this wood is connected to Fugue," Ferris whispered. "Look closer and you'll see the keys are missing."

Fiona crossed the clearing. The oak tree seemed to grow with every step she took. She approached the piano and opened the fallboard to reveal where a keyboard should have been, but Ferris was right. It was empty.

"Of all the letters I found on the trees, I never saw one after G, just as the keys on a piano are A through G."

Fiona marveled at this. All this time, while she was stuck at home playing scales, this grand glittering instrument was just beyond her reach. Even without the keys, the piano was striking. It was a light maple wood that appeared bright against the bark of the oak tree. The upper panel was inlaid with golden instruments that flashed as if part of an orchestra conducted by the moon.

Ferris hopped off Fiona's shoulder and into the keybed. Then he disappeared into the belly of the piano. His voice echoed. "That block, as you're calling it, is a key. Put it in the keybed, and I'll fix the piano from here."

Chapter 6

Fiona took what she now recognized was not a block but a piano key out of her breast pocket. She laid it in the left side of the keybed, somewhere between the lowest note and Middle C. She couldn't explain why, but she felt the key belonged there. She found herself wondering, if this was the key to Fugue, where did the other eighty-seven keys lead? And were they all hidden in her backyard?

"All set," she said, keeping her voice low. She didn't like the idea of being the loudest thing in the woods. She'd been able to clear her mind of the shadowy figure in the light of day. But now, in the middle of the forest, anything could be hidden among the trees.

Ferris popped out of the piano. He looked up at Fiona with a toothless smile. "It's ready."

Fiona laid her finger gently on the key. A deep, resounding tone rang through the forest. The note bounced off the trees and surrounded Fiona like a cocoon. It took hold in her mind and buzzed around inside it. It was a C, but a deeper one than the note that had interrupted her piano lesson. Still, this piano had to be responsible for the music in the trees. But who would play a piano in the middle of the woods?

The note lingered for a few seconds, then grew quieter and finally was gone.

"What now?" Fiona asked.

Ferris looked around as if the answer would appear before them. He hesitated. "I've never gotten this far. I don't know what comes next."

"Should I try again?" Fiona asked.

The frog nodded. "Press the key with more force this time."

Fiona pressed the key with a stronger touch. Again, the sound reverberated. Only this time, instead of swimming around her head, Fiona thought she could hear the note traveling in a certain direction. It was louder in her left ear than in her right. "Maybe we should follow the sound," she said, loudly enough that Ferris could hear over the note.

Ferris agreed and hopped on Fiona's shoulder so they could follow it. This time Fiona led the way through the forest. Without Ferris guiding her, she took smaller, more careful steps. She lifted her feet to avoid tripping and held her hands in front of her in case she did. Every few steps, she stopped to check if she could still hear the note, not sure she could get back to the piano if she made a wrong turn. But the note lasted much longer than any she played on her piano at home.

At last, her outstretched hands met a tree. She felt a gentle vibration in the tips of her fingers. The note faded.

"We're here," she said as the note ended. "Wherever here is."

For a moment, the woods were quiet once again. Then a low rumble began under Fiona's feet. The bark of the tree cracked and slid open, revealing a small door.

"Ha!" Ferris laughed. "A hidden door. There is more magic here than I thought."

He hopped off Fiona's shoulder and crawled towards the door. He looked back and said simply, "Are you ready?"

Fiona hesitated. Her mother's rules played like movie credits in her mind. Would it be alright to disappear into a magical door? Maybe she could just leave Ferris here now that they had found a way for him to get home. The frog hopped impatiently. Fiona had to admit she was curious. Maybe she'd just take a peek.

The opening in the tree was just big enough for Fiona to walk through without ducking. Her flashlight flickered as she passed through the doorway. The tree seemed to be sucking the light out of it in a battle for the darkness. After a few struggling flashes, the tree won the battle and the flashlight shut off. Fiona held her breath and blinked. She hoped her eyes would adjust, but there was nothing for them to adjust to. There was no place darker than inside a tree.

Ferris reassured Fiona. "The darkness doesn't last long. We just have to get through the tree, and Fugue will be on the other side."

Fiona shuffled forward, not sure it would be any easier to see in the Fugue fog. But after one more step, sunlight nearly blinded her. "This can't be—" she started.

"No. Definitely not Fugue," replied Ferris.

Fiona and Ferris stood on an empty narrow sidewalk. In front of them was just the opposite. A wide, busy street carried crowds of vehicles that zipped or meandered. Some drove on the road, some rode above it on an invisible highway suspended in air. Fiona felt like she was watching an ever-changing merry-go-round. No two vehicles were the same. An athlete pedaled a robotic hammock. A nurse gripped the string of a balloon. There were mechanical animals—a towering bronze ostrich, a bedazzled beetle, a steel grizzly bear. Ferris scoffed at the man sitting atop a copper frog. "Suppose I'll use humans as transportation when I get home."

The left side of Fiona's mouth rose into a smirk. Wasn't that exactly what he'd been doing in the woods? Fiona was the car and Ferris its passenger. She would've walked backwards had he told her to go in reverse.

Over her shoulder, the woods Fiona had longed to explore for eleven years were gone. There was only a single tree, the one they'd used to enter this place. It was decorated with an ornate silver arch. The phrase "Discovery Awaits" was written in bold at the top of it.

"I think we need to ask for directions," Fiona said, placing Ferris on her shoulder and stepping to the edge of the sidewalk. She was nervous in this odd place among strangers, but having no plan of action was even more uncomfortable. Fiona called out to a teenager piloting a paper airplane. They didn't notice her. She called out to a couple in a bird's nest. They couldn't hear her over their conversation.

A caterpillar school bus inched down the road. The children in the middle of the bus bounced up and down as the center of the caterpillar rose and fell. A teacher stood at the front of the insect, which appeared to be the least bouncy place, and announced, "I hope you remembered your thinking caps! Today we decide our curriculum for the semester. What do you want to learn?"

In Fiona's experience, teachers were patient and reliable sources of information. She breathed a sigh of relief as she waved towards the bus to ask for directions. She was about to speak when the students began to shout their answers.

"How to build a rocket ship!"

"What's a black hole?"

"Why do bubbles pop?"

For a moment, Fiona wanted to join the students on the bus. She too was curious why bubbles pop. It probably had something to do with pressure.

She caught the distracted glance of a student. His eyes lingered on Fiona for a moment before turning back to his teacher. A sinking feeling reminded her that even in this world, her spots probably wouldn't fit in. She shook her curls in front of her face to hide the blemishes.

Ferris tugged at a strand of Fiona's hair. "Let's try something else."

The pair walked down the street to find someone who wasn't in a moving contraption. Down the road, they found a row of storefronts. Fiona looked for a school or a firehouse. She knew those were good places to go if she was ever lost. And she was definitely lost. Instead, she saw curious shop signs. They were certainly not the kind of places she had back home. *Android Psychology*, *Quantum Friendships*, *Nanobody Matchmaking* the signs read as she walked. Her head spun as she tried to figure out what those things meant.

They finally came upon a familiar type of storefront. On display in a bay window sat a three-tiered cake. It was decorated with soft white icing and dotted with green cupcakes sticking out at odd angles.

In an explosion of frosting, the cupcakes burst from the cake. Fiona's shoulders tensed. Then the cupcakes twirled in the air like figure skaters. All at once, they retracted back into the cake as if nothing had happened. They were controlled by an almost imperceptible mechanical device.

The name *Arti Glen's Cakery* was etched in the glass window. With Ferris on her shoulder, Fiona pushed open the door. A bell jingled above her head. She crossed the tile floor to a glass counter full of elaborately decorated cakes and called out, "Hello?"

A slender boy in a lavender suit ducked out from behind a curtain at the back of the shop. He had pale, unkempt hair, and flour stuck to his cheek. "Welcome to Arti Glen's Cakery!" he said merrily. "I'm Arti. Can I interest you in a sample?"

Ferris perked up. "Do you have any cricket?"

"Cricket? No. Never cared for them myself, but I do have grasshopper pops if you'd like a taste." Arti maneuvered around the counter, a platter of cakes in hand. "They're very hoppy." He winked, extending the platter towards Ferris.

Though Arti was a good foot taller than Fiona, he couldn't have been much older than she was. "Did your parents name the bakery after you?" she asked.

Arti cocked his head. "My parents? No. I named the bakery after myself."

"You own it?" Fiona couldn't quite believe that. "Aren't you young to have your own business?"

Arti stood up taller, looking more confused than hurt by the question. "Fourteen is perfectly old enough."

Fiona was puzzled. At home, it was possible to get a job at fourteen, but to own a business was something else entirely. She wanted to ask more about it, but her words stuck in her throat. What if Arti looked at her spots the way the boy on the bus had? She lowered her chin and let her curls fall over her face as she mulled over the cake samples on the platter. Each piece of cake had a toothpick with a flag label stuck into it. She was not interested in the Avocado Cream Cheese or the Grape Raisin.

"Birthday cabbage?" she asked quizzically.

"For the rabbits of course, though the vegans enjoy it too." Arti replied, smiling from ear to ear.

There were so many choices. Fiona tried to carefully consider them all, but she was conscious of Ferris and Arti staring at her. She finally chose a flavor she could at least wrap her head around—a square of Chocolate Popcorn cake. Gooey frosting stuck to her fingers. The cake itself was dense and moist, but the popcorn left a cheesy flavor in her mouth, so she picked it off and ate it separately.

"Can you point us in the direction of Fugue?" Ferris asked.

Arti put the cake platter on the counter. He crossed his arms and pursed his lips in thought. Then he stood on his head. "I think better this way," Arti explained. It seemed to work because only a few seconds later, he concluded, "The only direction I can point you in is out the way you came. This isn't Fugue, and you can't get there from the tree you entered."

Fiona glanced at Ferris with concern. His face fell.

Arti let his feet fall to the ground and stood upright. "But this *is* Electronica where discovery awaits! I'm sure someone here has been to Fugue. In fact, I'm catering a party tonight for a well-traveled friend. Come with me and I'll introduce you to him."

Fiona looked around for a clock, not sure how long she could stay out without her parents noticing. "How long will that take?" she asked. "I left home without telling my parents. I don't want them to worry about me."

"First time through a tree portal?" asked Arti, tapping his nose knowingly.

Fiona nodded. Somehow, she was already feeling more comfortable around Arti. He hadn't blinked twice at the iridescent talking frog. She didn't think he'd care about some red splotches. "I'm from Massachusetts."

"Of course, Moose Achoo Suits. I've heard of it." He clearly hadn't. "Well, you don't have to worry about time just yet. I suppose you could worry about it, but it wouldn't do you any good. Totally different time zones. The lands within the trees are one hundred fifty-six hours behind Moose... where you're from. As long as you don't stay more than a week, you'll return at the same time you left. It's a helpful trick for traveling through worlds."

Fiona didn't think that was how time zones worked, but she hadn't thought talking frogs or tree portals or magic pianos existed until now either, so she didn't question it.

"How many worlds are there?" asked Ferris.

"Got to be at least eighty-eight, " Arti replied. "One for each key."

Fiona straightened. If the piano had once had a full keybed, that could explain why the dream she'd had about the woods had felt so real. Maybe she'd been allowed in the woods as a child. Maybe she knew about the piano and its notes. It didn't seem likely. But what if the reason she wasn't allowed in the woods was because something had happened to her? Something worse than ticks or getting lost.

Ferris slumped his head on Fiona's shoulder. Fiona could practically see what he was thinking. There were eighty-eight worlds, and he had no idea how to get home. The frog closed his eyes as if to shut out the thought, and Fiona laid him in a sunny spot in the window to rest.

"The piano was empty when we got to it. What happened to the rest of the keys?" Fiona asked.

"Would you like to stand on your head while I tell you the story? It's good for listening too." Arti said, looking so encouragingly at Fiona that she considered it. But she never had been good at handstands. She shook her head.

A metal table with two wobbly chairs sat empty on the cakery floor. Arti pulled one of the chairs out from the table. Fiona thought he meant for her to sit in it, but then he dragged the chair across the floor and threw it forcefully behind the curtain. "No need for these really," Arti said, dragging the second chair out of the room. "No one can listen while sitting still." Something crashed in the kitchen as he threw the other chair. "Anyway, good stories are told from rooftops and mountains, not chairs." Arti tapped the table for Fiona to sit on and she hopped up onto it. He sat cross-legged on the counter beside his cakes like they, too, were going to listen to his story.

Chapter 7

There was a time when the Great Piano had all of its keys. Travel between worlds was simple. The Piano Commission oversaw visitor relations and upkeep. It was made up of four elected officials, each with unique abilities to care for the piano. The only rule was that no two commissioners could be from the same world. Giants shared the responsibility with leprechauns. Mermaids shared with sailors. The Commission tuned the piano each night, allowing travelers to reach their destinations with ease.

But there were some who didn't like visitors. At first, they only whispered concerns to their friends. "We should close the portals," they said. And when their friends agreed, they told their neighbors. The idea spread like a trickling faucet, one drip at a time that no one gave any thought to until there was suddenly a flood. Soon the concerned ones were holding rallies. They chanted, "Close the gates! Close the gates!" They surrounded the piano and blocked travelers from playing it.

They got on the interworldly news and spread fear that entire communities would be lost if the worlds remained open to all. "What would happen," they said, "if the Fugue frogs experienced the sunshine of Electronica? Would anyone still want to live by the dark, damp pond? Worse still," they said, "what would happen if the Symphony snakes moved to Fugue? Frogs would have to go into hiding or be eaten. Who knows how many would survive?"

It was easier to manipulate worlds if the citizens had more to lose. Frogs have many predators, so Fugue was an easy target. But the fear was just fear and nothing else. There was no evidence that frogs were leaving home for the sunshine and no evidence that snakes wanted anything to do with Fugue. Travelers weren't abandoning their homes. They were learning from other worlds, and each world was more prosperous because of what they learned from the others.

Nevertheless, the fear took hold. It slithered between worlds and wrapped itself around anyone it could, squeezing them tighter and tighter until they were paralyzed with fear. Keys went missing from the piano, taken by the fearful. The Piano Commission made new keys. It wasn't an easy task; key making is a fine art. But the new keys went missing too.

After months and months of missing keys, the commission grew tired of making new ones. They disbanded, and as their last act, they gave the keys to the leaders of each world to let them decide what to do with them.

"That is why some worlds," said Arti, whispering to the cakes, "are more open than others. The people of Electronica value invention—discovery! It's difficult to discover without exploration." Arti looked up at Fiona like he'd just remembered she was there. "Seeing as we don't have a singular leader, we took it upon ourselves to create our own keys and share them. Several keys exist to enter Electronica. They're not as good as the ones the commission used to make. Sometimes they're a bit out of tune, but they usually work well enough. It's not uncommon for Electronicans to have keys to other open worlds either.

"Fugue, on the other hand"—Arti nodded towards Ferris and lowered his voice once more—"is nearly impossible to get into. Their world has been closed off for so long, many frogs don't even know about the piano. You'll need help getting there. If anyone knows how, it will be Torien Umba. I'm sure he could help you, but he won't let us into his party empty handed." Arti scratched his head. "And I have to admit, I've been procrastinating. I have to deliver a cake within the hour."

"An hour?" Fiona asked. That was no time at all to bake a cake. Sometimes it took her an hour just to decide what kind of cake she wanted to eat.

"Yes, well, I think my procrastinating paid off. You're here now, so you can help... Please." Arti hopped off the counter and held back the curtain at the back of the shop. With a wave of his arm, he invited Fiona to walk through it. She bit her cheek. She hoped this boy knew what he was doing. What if Torien didn't know how to get to Fugue? What if this party was a waste of Ferris's time? This world was unlike any place she'd ever known, she wanted to learn more about it. But she couldn't waste time baking while Ferris was separated from his family. She couldn't forget she was the one who'd kept him from them. She looked towards the frog in the window. He was fast asleep. Maybe an hour couldn't hurt.

The kitchen of Arti Glen's Cakery was barely wide enough to fit an oven. If Fiona had wanted to lie across it, she would have to sleep in the fetal position or else her feet would kick one side while her head hit the other. But the room was at least six ovens long and had very high ceilings. If Fiona could sleep standing up, she would never hit the ceiling unless she grew to be fifty feet tall.

Leaning against the walls were two ladders that reached at least three stories high. Arti's baking equipment was nailed precariously overhead. The chairs he had thrown were toppled over at the back of the narrow room. "It's not much," Arti said, plucking a pair of plum aprons off a hook on the wall. "But the closeness keeps my thoughts in." He squeezed the air around his head and handed Fiona the smaller apron.

A mixer shook violently on the wall nearest Fiona. She was careful not to stand directly under it.

"I've tried three times this week to make a pineapple upside down cake. Every time I flip it over, it falls on the floor," Arti lamented.

"You're not supposed to—" Fiona tried to interrupt.

"—so I need a sparkling new idea! What have you got?"

Fiona thought for a moment. "How about flan?"

Arti shook his head. "I made flan for Torien's birthday last month—the man has a lot of parties. But any great cake engineer must be up for a challenge! What else? What did you have for lunch?"

Fiona thought for a moment. The last lunch she'd had was leftover omelets after her recital. Her heart panged to remember it. It felt so long ago. She wished her mom could see this world. Her mom was braver than Fiona, probably brave enough to try the grape raisin cake. "I had sesame chicken omelets," Fiona replied.

Arti flinched. "Yikes!—Sorry—No, that won't work, but to each their own! Anything else? Did you have anything interesting for dinner last night? An unusual snack, perhaps?"

Remembering the snack she'd found in her jacket, Fiona reached into her upper right pocket and pulled out a pack of gummy fruit snacks. "What about these?"

Arti took the crinkly wrapper from Fiona and inspected it. He tore open the package and poured a few gummies into his hand. He rolled them around, squished an orange one between his fingers, then popped the handful into his mouth.

"I see," he said, sucking at his teeth. "It's a miniature fruit salad, but each fruit has the same texture."

"Gummies," corrected Fiona.

"Oh, how fun! Gummies! Yes, this could definitely work."

Arti ascended a ladder and began pulling tins of various sizes off the wall and dropping them on the floor. There were enough to make a ten-layer gummy cake. "That door there," Arti pointed. "Could you pick out ten fruits from the walk-in?"

Fiona pulled open the bulky silver door Arti had pointed to. She had never been in a walk-in refrigerator before. It was a chilly room with ingredients held in neatly organized plastic containers. It hummed a comforting G note. Fiona surprised herself with the thought. She hadn't been able to identify notes this easily before. Maybe all that time practicing scales had actually paid off.

The refrigerator door thudded behind Fiona. Her eyes widened. Was she supposed to have put something in front of the door to keep it from closing? She quickly pushed on the slab of metal, checking she wasn't locked in the room. She breathed a sigh of relief to see the door opened easily. Though the chill of touching it sent goosebumps crawling up her arm. She was glad to have her jacket.

Fiona browsed the selection of fruits located conveniently on the bottom shelf. Though she sometimes helped with the cooking at home, her mom always chose what to make. She didn't want to mess this up. She carefully examined the wide variety of ingredients. There were buckets of every fruit imaginable, and even some that were unimaginable. Fiona chewed her bottom lip as she tried to think what an adventurous Electronican would want to have at his party. She pulled a few containers off the shelves labeled *Durian* and *Cherimoya*, then she put them back. Finally, she chose colors and flavors she thought would go well together.

One by one she stacked the containers of chopped fruits into her arms. Cranberry, strawberry, clementine, lemon, mango, kiwi, lime, blueberry, blackberry, and tamarind. Almost a perfect rainbow. The containers were stacked well above her head. She struggled to balance them as she re-entered the kitchen.

"All right, throw them up here!" Arti called.

Fiona looked from top to bottom at the stack of fruit she had chosen. "All at once?" she asked.

"Of course! We don't have time to be cautious. There's a reason they teach acrobatics in school." Arti leapt to the second ladder, a few rungs down from where he had been before.

"They don't teach acrobatics at my school," Fiona said, walking the fruit to Arti. "What kind of school did you go to?"

Arti shrugged. "An ordinary one." He took the containers from Fiona and tossed the fruit through the air, making the rainbow Fiona had hoped for. Each fruit landed in its own blender at a different height on the wall. "If they don't teach acrobatics, you must at least have zero gravity lessons?"

"No. We—we have spelling and math," Fiona replied. She couldn't help but wonder about the zero gravity lessons. Were they held in space? Did students need a special permission slip to go? Her classmates were always asking when they'd use the math they were learning, but certainly math was more useful than zero gravity.

"Spelling?" Arti guffawed. He scaled the ladder and put his knees over the highest rung. He bent over backwards to reach a jar of honey and a can of apple juice. While still upside down, he asked, "Do you just sit in a chair and write down a list of words?"

Fiona nodded.

"Do you at least get to pick the words?" Arti jumped from blender to blender, adding a dash of honey and a splash of juice.

Fiona shook her head no.

"What an odd school. How does anyone learn to think for themselves?"

Fiona didn't know how to answer that. Instead, she organized the ten tins Arti had pulled from the wall onto a very narrow table. Actually, it wasn't quite a table. It was more like a plank of wood. "Is learning to think for yourself something you have to do on your own?" Fiona asked, hoping maybe the time she spent alone was good for her.

"I don't think so," said Arti, balancing a box of gelatin powder on his toes. He kicked the box and gelatin fell like snow into the fruit-filled blenders. "The best way to think for yourself is to get every viewpoint—speaking of which, could you hop on that ladder and pour the fruit into tins?"

Fiona climbed the ladder opposite Arti. She reached the third rung and took the crimson cranberry mixture from the wall. She started to carefully climb back down the ladder.

"Stop right there," Arti grinned. "We only go up. Changing viewpoints, remember?" Fiona wanted to explain that it wasn't safe to multitask while on a ladder, but Arti quickly added, "Plus we only have forty-five minutes to get to Torien's now.

"Right," Fiona said, glancing nervously at the blenders that hung well above her. "Only up then."

Arti nodded encouragingly. From the third rung, Fiona leaned over and poured the cranberry puree into the tin on the table. Almost half of the mix splattered onto the floor. Her eyes flicked anxiously towards Arti.

"Holy fruitcakes," he cheered. "Look what you made. One big cake and seven mini ones! I wonder how many

I can make." Arti poured the clementine puree from one story above the floor. It splattered around the tin. "Ten!" he shouted.

Fiona giggled and climbed up the ladder, pouring the strawberry, mango, kiwi, and blackberry mixtures onto the tins below. They all splattered. The floor was a mess, but it was beautiful too. "Some of the splatters mixed together," Fiona said. "Do you think the guests would like cranberry mango?"

Arti was almost drooling. "If they have taste buds they will." He slid down the ladder. "And look, you never would have made those from down here," Arti said as Fiona descended back down the ladder.

"Are you worried about germs?" Fiona asked.

Arti pondered the question. "Not generally."

"I mean because of the cakes," she clarified. "They're on the floor."

"Oh, yes. They are. But I asked the infectious bacteria not to enter this kitchen. There are microscopic signs at the entrance. Bacteria may not take spelling lessons, but they can still read. They're very polite actually."

Arti stacked the cakes from large to small, leaving a few of the more awkward-shaped ones aside. He looked the cake up and down. "I think we have a few minutes for finishing touches. Do you want to add anything?"

FIONA AND THE FORGOTTEN PIANO

Fiona didn't want to let the odd little cakes go to waste. She weaved the squishy gummies together to form a basket and balanced it at the very top of the cake. It now stood as tall as she did.

Arti clapped. "An upside-down fruit basket is more wondrous than an upside-down pineapple cake could ever be. Thank you… " Arti's face contorted. He scratched his chin. "Breadsticks! I never learned your name."

Chapter 8

Fiona made her way to the front of the shop. Ferris's eyes were open. He sat quietly watching Electronicans pass by the window. He wasn't grumbling so Fiona reasoned he must've been in better spirits. She carried him to the kitchen. Upon seeing the cake, Ferris stretched his legs. He leaned towards the dessert with squinted eyes. "Any of those layers worm flavored?"

"All fruit I'm afraid," Arti replied.

Ferris grunted.

"I bet there'll be worm waffles at the party," Arti said hurriedly in a clear attempt to please Ferris. "The guests are probably munching on appetizers right now. We should get going." Arti boxed up the cake and placed it onto a rolling cart, which he wheeled to the back parking lot. Leaning against a brick wall at the back of the bakery was Arti's ride.

"We're taking a bike to the party?" asked Fiona.

Arti scratched the back of his neck. Roses bloomed in his cheeks. "I don't have a license to operate autonomous vehicles, but there's plenty of room for all of us on this trusty device."

Fiona couldn't see how two humans, a frog, and a very large cake could fit on the insubstantial bike, but she was swiftly proven wrong when Arti pulled a small remote from his suit pocket. He clicked a few buttons and the bike whirled to life. It straightened itself off the wall and wheeled around in front of them. Arti pressed a few more buttons. The bike extended, transforming into a tandem bike. It then grew four mechanical arms, two on each side of the bike's back seat.

Arti turned to Fiona. "We need to balance the bike. I'm thinking you on one arm and the cake on the other? Unless you want to drive?"

"I'm good on the arm," Fiona said, curious what Arti did to balance the bike when he worked alone.

Arti placed the cake on one side of the bike while Fiona sat on the other. Then he took the front seat. "Lots of options for you, Ferris. You've got two arms and a seat to choose from."

Ferris eyed the bike's gangly arms suspiciously and opted for the back seat. "What about helmets?" he grumbled.

"Helmets!" Arti laughed. "Good one, Ferris. This isn't the nineteen eighties. We've got force fields now."

Ferris mumbled something rude under his breath, and Arti began to pedal.

The ride through Electronica was smoother than any of Fiona's trips to school. She was used to her mother's minivan, which seemed to hit every pothole even if the pothole was in the opposite lane. But, as shaky as Arti's bike appeared, it felt as though it was floating on air. It navigated the crowded streets with ease and even did most of the pedaling.

Despite the traffic, the air was cleaner than any Fiona had experienced. She took a deep breath, letting the cool oxygen fill her lungs. She could smell tulips though there weren't any nearby. She didn't even know how she knew it was tulips and not roses she was smelling, but somehow the air made the scents more distinct.

Ferris actually appeared to be enjoying the ride. When he thought no one was looking, he let himself smile. Fiona saw it though. And she had a feeling he was smelling insects in the grass.

"Did you always want to be a baker?" Fiona asked Arti.

"My family is all material scientists. I was supposed to be one too," he shouted over the traffic. "They thought I'd enjoy generating new building materials or dreaming up ways to carry medicine that never expires." Arti steered off the main street and onto a quieter road, but he didn't lower his voice. Perhaps he thought anecdotes were better told loudly. "For my last assignment, I thought, what if I could make a window that wouldn't hurt if you fell through it? Wouldn't it be even more fun if it were bouncy like a trampoline?" Arti lifted his elbows like he was about to pop a wheelie, but he thought better of it. "I made flexible glass, but instead of melting sand, as one usually does, I melted sugar. I stayed up until two a.m. every night for a week before it was due. In the end, I had made butterscotch, mocha, and creamsicle glass. Fun, but not very useful as a building material. I got a C on the project. However, when I convinced my teachers to take a bite of the glass, it was so delicious they bumped my grade up to a B. I opened up my cakery one week later, and I've worked there ever since."

Fiona wondered how Arti had convinced his teachers to eat glass. It seemed a rather dangerous thing. "I'd love to try the glass sometime," she said, though she knew she'd only be brave enough to lick it. Arti looked over his right shoulder and winked.

The bike turned left onto a residential road. The houses—if you could call them that—were as unique as the vehicles of Electronica. She found herself playing a game of Goldilocks in search of the perfect one. That house was too dangerous, that one too... fuzzy?

A cylindrical home hovered above the ground like a spaceship preparing to land. How did the homeowners get out of it? Was there a slide? A rope? Maybe they were acrobats too.

They passed a greenhouse built with woven vines of cucumber and squash. Fiona frowned thinking of all the meals her mother would make her eat if she lived there. Cucumber and squash salad. Cucumber and squash soup. Cucumber and squash pancakes. It wasn't the house for her. Maybe it would be okay if it grew melons.

Someone had brought down a cloud from the sky. Every once in a while, a brunette head peeked out of the white fluff like it was a game of whack-a-mole. How the person managed to see through the cloud was a mystery. They must trip on table legs all the time.

None of the houses were quite right, which, Fiona supposed, was okay because she didn't live in any of them.

After one final turn, Arti abruptly powered off the bike with a STOP button between the handlebars. Fiona jerked forward in her seat and the force field gently lifted her back into place. "Are we here?" she asked doubtfully.

They had stopped in front of a set of rusty train tracks at the bottom of a steep hill. There were no more houses around, only mossy boulders and overgrown foliage.

"Almost," replied Arti as he leaned over to pull on a worn copper lever next to the tracks.

The lever clicked into place.

A short-statured robot with wheels for eyes and springs for a nose popped its head out from behind a rock. It clinked and clacked its way towards Arti. The robot stood only about as high as Fiona's knees. She found herself resisting the urge to lift the robot up and say *Aren't you just the cutest?* in the same voice she used to speak to puppies.

"Hello Mr. Glen, do you need a lift to Torien's house?" the robot asked. She had the voice of a fragile old woman. Fiona was relieved she hadn't tried to pick her up.

"Thank you, Dorothy, that would be superfluous." Arti cleared his throat. "Nope, sorry, not the right word. I've been upright far too long. I meant to say that would be superb."

Dorothy smiled sweetly. "Care to try the roller coaster setting today?" she asked, tottering over to a dial embedded in the ground.

"Oh—uh—no, thank you. Maybe I'll work up the courage next time. Anyway, we've brought cake and wouldn't want it to apple—ahem—topple."

"Yes, Mr. Glen. I'll change the setting to *walking like you've got a cup of hot chocolate filled to the brim*." Dorothy placed her robotic arm on the dial and turned it three clicks.

Arti let out a sigh of relief. "That sounds tranquil enough."

From around the bend, a pair of vintage roller skates the size of train cars rolled down the tracks. They slowed to a halt in front of Dorothy. "Hop in everyone. I'm sure Torien is growing impatient for your arrival."

Each skate had twelve seats, six on each side where the shoelaces tucked in. Fiona climbed the buckles of the roller skate closest to her and took a seat in a middle row. She adjusted the shoelace like a seat belt. Ferris hopped off the bike and chose a seat at the front of the skate. She admired his confidence. Fiona had never been brave enough to take the first row of anything.

In the time it took Fiona to sit down, Dorothy had wrapped the bike and the cake safely away in the shoelace of the other skate. She was now attempting to strap Arti in, but he was making it difficult by sitting with his head tucked between his knees.

Arti waved his hand in the air. "Don't worry about me, Dorothy. Just waiting for the blood to return to my brain. I'm not worried about these rackety old skates at all. They're perfectly safe. Perfectly old and rickety and safe."

Fiona raised an eyebrow, confused by Arti's apparent nerves. This was a boy who did acrobatics while he baked. Surely these sturdy skates were safer than his flimsy self-driving bike.

Dorothy gave up. Arti could strap himself in. She shuffled back to the copper lever. "See you in a few hours Mr. Glen," Dorothy called, pulling the lever.

A trap door at the front of the skate flipped open. From the door arose a mug of hot chocolate, filled to the brim.

The skate's wheels began to turn. Fiona's seat began to vibrate. It was pleasant at first, like a massage chair, but as the skates turned uphill, the shaking became violent. The tracks went every which way but straight. They dipped below a rushing river and stumbled through thorny shrubs. With each bump, Fiona's seat belt loosened around her torso. She tried forcing it back into the slit in the seat from where it came, but she couldn't get it back into place. She wrapped her hands around the bottom of her seat to keep from bouncing out of it.

Thwack! Fiona was struck by a low hanging tree branch. Her cheekbone stung. But she couldn't lift her hand to wipe the pain away without risking falling out of the skates. She scooted down as far as she could and managed a glance at Ferris. His body rattled, but his sticky feet protected him from bouncing.

Curiously, the hot chocolate on the toe of the skate stood perfectly still. How was it doing that? Was it sitting on a shock resistant platform?

The skates hit a boulder. Fiona's grip loosened.

They hit another. Fiona's seatbelt smacked against the side of the skate.

One more hit like that and— Fiona lost her grip. She flew out of her seat. She was sent careening through the air. The skates raced off without her. Ferris and Arti didn't look back. They didn't know she'd been rocketed from the skate.

Fiona landed with a thump in a mud puddle. Her perfectly clean pajamas were splatter painted brown. Fiona's first thought should have been *Am I okay?* Instead, it was, *What will everyone think if I show up with brown stains on my pants?* She looked around for a way to clean herself and remembered the river they'd passed. Surely showing up wet was better than showing up muddy. She walked sideways down the hill, remembering from hikes with her father that walking sideways was the safest way to descend without slipping. Her sneakers sunk into the leafy ground. When she reached the river, Fiona held her hands together to make a bowl. She scooped a handful of water onto her pants. Now she was wet and muddy.

Fiona bit her lip, wondering if there was any way around what she was about to do. When she couldn't think of anything, she sighed and sat in the river.

Chapter 9

Fiona let the cold water wash over her pants, rubbing the mud away. When she stood, she was pleasantly surprised at how much mud she was able to remove. The wet pants were a new issue, but hopefully they would dry as she walked. She found her way back to where she had fallen and followed the rusty skate tracks up the hill, leaving a trail of water behind her.

When Fiona saw the glass house, she knew it was Torien's. Not only because the roller skates were sitting outside of it, but also because it was so large that three of her houses would have fit inside. The home was tinted pink as the sun set behind it. Dark figures moved about on the first floor and faint classical music filled the air. From the driveway, Fiona could see that several of the rooms had screens for walls. But the most unusual thing about the house was its foundation. Rather than one of stone or brick, the house sat on giant rotating gears.

Arti ran to Fiona in a panic. "Oh, my ganache! Are you okay?" He placed his hands on Fiona's shoulders and spun her around to get a good look at her. "We were so terribly worried. These roller skates can be quite the nasty ride."

Ferris crawled to Fiona's side. "Could've warned us before we got on them," he scowled, wringing out water from the hem in Fiona's pant leg. Fiona's heart warmed at the sweet gesture.

"I'm fine, really," she said.

"I feel like curdled cake batter," Arti said. "I just get so terribly nervous around those rolling contraptions I can't think of anything else."

"I'll pick the setting when we leave," said Ferris. It wasn't a question. Fiona held her breath.

"Of course, of course," Arti nodded. He trembled as he lifted the cake out of the skates. Fiona thought his shaking hands weren't from the weight of the cake but from lingering jitters. She thought about asking if he should do a cartwheel or balance on one foot or whatever other strange thing Arti might believe could help in this particular situation. Instead, she stepped in to help carry the cake.

"Why did the skates go so fast when the setting was supposed to be walking with a cup of hot chocolate?" she asked, taking one side of the cake box in her hands.

"I wondered that myself," said Arti. He tilted his head around the box to explain. "Apparently that hot chocolate has been sitting in the skate since it was made. I tried to stick my finger in it, but it's as hard as rock candy."

Fiona scratched her head. How long did hot chocolate have to sit before it became rock solid? It had to be years, possibly decades. The cup was probably more mold than chocolate. She was glad she hadn't been the one to inspect it. "So... the skates moved like that because no matter how fast they went, the hot chocolate never spilled?"

"Yes, it's exactly that. The sensors didn't pick up on any movement in the hot chocolate cup. The skates had no reason to slow down."

Arti and Fiona shuffled sideways up the stairs to Torien's house. Ferris hopped on Fiona's head and flicked his tongue out to ring the doorbell. The door swung open immediately, though no one was behind it. A charming voice from a speaker overhead said, "Welcome Arti and uninvited guests. You're seven and a half minutes late."

Arti winced. He already wasn't having the best day. The sass from Torien's advanced security system wasn't helping. "This cake is worth the wait. I promise you that," he said with false cheer. It seemed Arti needed to make everyone happy, even the virtual assistants. At home, Fiona's mother had no trouble yelling at the little voice on her phone. *No Sara, I already know tomorrow's weather. I need to know if it rained last week.* But her mother's phone wasn't named Sara, so it didn't answer.

Fiona, Ferris, and Arti found themselves in an underwhelming kitchen. The view of the hill was pleasant, but the cabinetry and appliances were a utilitarian gray. The room had a distinct lack of personality. Fiona and Arti placed the cake gently on the kitchen island.

"Go enjoy the party," said Arti. "I just have to unbox the cake. I'll be right out."

The speakers that greeted them now sang pleasant jazz music. A murmur of voices came from the doorway adjacent to the kitchen. Fiona swallowed. She wasn't particularly keen on entering large rooms full of people. She never knew how they'd react to her spots. She could only hope the room was filled with other Arti's. Not literally though because that would be creepy, and Electronicans probably did have the ability to make human clones. She amended her internal thoughts to say that she hoped the room was filled with people *like* Arti.

The room next door was open and spacious. It looked like it should be a living room, but there were very few things in it—no couches or chairs or bookshelves or lamps. What was in the room were people. People congregating at high top tables. People sitting on museum benches, and people watching nature scenes playing out on the screen walls.

Fiona took a deep breath. It was unlikely she'd get through this party, or even the next five minutes, without someone making a rude comment about her spots. But while her feet wanted to stay put, her stomach betrayed her. It growled ferociously. Fiona couldn't just stand at the edge of the room. She had to at least try the appetizers. She placed a hand on her stomach to quiet it and sidled up to a mostly empty table which held a platter of juicy watermelon cheese cubes. She gulped down four of them.

Nestled in her hair, Ferris reached down and tapped Fiona on the forehead. Fiona jerked her head back. She'd forgotten the frog was there. "Glad you're enjoying yourself, but I'm going to go look for those worm waffles," he said, hopping out of Fiona's hair and over to another table.

The party guests were dressed in ruffles and floral print suits. Fiona pinched her muddy cotton pajama pants between her fingers. She wished she were wearing something nicer. But when she glanced at a few of the faces in the room she noticed she didn't stand out nearly as much as she thought she would. Electronicans seemed more daring with their makeup than anyone back home. Some wore crowns of silver sparkles across their foreheads like they'd been grazed by a shooting star. Others painted scales on their cheeks like they'd swum straight out of the sea. There were even a few folks who had an extra set of eyes drawn on their cheeks. It was no wonder Arti hadn't mentioned Fiona's freckles. Here, they were decorative. Feeling a bit more at ease, Fiona made her way to a busier table where the guests were engrossed in conversation.

"If we could stimulate jaw bones to grow a third set of teeth, there would be no need for dentures," quipped a dentist. Fiona moved her tongue over the back of her teeth. Three sets of teeth seemed like too many for one mouth.

"Did you know tomatoes have seven thousand more genes than humans? Imagine the flavors and nutritional benefits we could put in them," remarked a farmer. Fiona scrunched her eyebrows together. Weren't tomatoes already healthy? Couldn't we turn brownies into vitamins instead?

"We could build mountain ranges each winter to slow the planet's rotation. That would mean more sunlight and no seasonal depression. It's a win-win!" said a construction worker. Now that was just impractical. But Fiona did appreciate the Electronican way of thinking. It seemed no idea was too outlandish. No one was laughed at for thinking up something strange or for being unique. She could get used to that.

"I don't believe we've been introduced." A woman with curious eyes interrupted Fiona's thoughts as she twirled the ice in her drink. Her forehead and left cheek were marked with a red snakeskin pattern. She stood with a confidence Fiona wished she had. The woman introduced herself as Ms. Acara, Torien's patent lawyer. "Are you an investor?" She glanced down at Fiona's damp pajamas and answered her own question. "Not by the look of it. An engineer then? Or an inventor?"

Fiona turned a shade of mauve. "I'm just a kid. I don't have a job," she replied.

"That's an old way of thinking. Children can be productive members of society just as much as adults, sometimes even more so."

"Right." Fiona nodded. "I guess I'm still figuring that out."

"While you're figuring that out, let me demonstrate Torien's newest technology. I don't suppose you've seen it yet?"

Fiona shook her head.

"Alright then, who would you like to visit? We are beta testing the technology with the mermaids of Cantata, the giants of Crescendo, and the perytons of Sonata. The choice is yours."

Fiona frowned. "I don't know what a peryton is."

"Why don't you ask then?"

Fiona hesitated. Ms. Acara's manners were not ones she was used to. She had a strange way of making Fiona feel simultaneously welcome and unwelcome. In the end, she did ask, "What's a peryton?"

"Wonderful. You mustn't let questions pile up in your head like junk mail. You've got to throw them out. Follow me. I'll show you what a peryton is."

Ms. Acara led Fiona to a screen on the far wall which was playing a scene from a forest in autumn. Orange and yellow leaves filled the trees, and crunchy brown ones covered the ground. She tapped the screen with her manicured finger.

A text bubble appeared. Within it, a sentence materialized one letter at a time.

"Would you like to start a conversation?" it read.

She tapped the screen again to select *Yes*.

As if Fiona had put on noise canceling headphones, the music and conversations in the room muffled. "What did you do?" she asked.

"It's called a Sound Bubble," Ms. Acara replied. "It establishes a quiet space for those wanting to have a conversation. It also prevents others from eavesdropping." She tapped her ear. "Tonight, Torien has combined the Sound Bubble with his previous invention, the Artificial Key—patent pending—which allows us to talk to other worlds without physically being there. Not all worlds accept the invitation to speak with us, but the citizens of Sonata are quite friendly."

Fiona cocked her head. She wondered how big a Sound Bubble could get. Was it possible the woods outside her home had been surrounded by one? Could that be the reason the trees had fallen silent? Ms. Acara was right. The questions were piling up in her head. She let one out, "Did Torien put a Sound Bubble around the woods?"

The space between Ms. Acara's eyebrows narrowed. "That would be an odd thing to do. Why do you ask?" It didn't really answer the question.

"I'm not part of this world," Fiona replied. "I live outside the woods." As she said the words, she felt a string tug at her heart. She realized a part of her wished she was from this world. A world where teenagers could run businesses. A world where she could be a baker or an engineer or an inventor just as she was now without having to wait until she was old enough to achieve those things.

Ms. Acara nodded. "Well, if someone put a Sound Bubble around the woods, I would know about it. They would have to license the technology from Torien. It would be a lot of paperwork. Lots of signatures. I don't think I would have missed a transaction like that."

Fiona's lips pinched together. If there wasn't a Sound Bubble around the woods, why did they suddenly become silent the night she left home? What else could do that? It didn't make sense. It seemed more likely someone had used the technology and neglected to tell Ms. Acara about it. Maybe Torien was using the Sound Bubble in ways Ms. Acara wasn't aware of. Fiona kept this thought to herself. She didn't think the lawyer would take it well. She was glad when she didn't have to change the subject.

A doe emerged from the left side of the screen. Autumnal leaves crunched beneath her feet, two of them hooved and two of them clawed. She had fleecy ears, gentle black eyes, and magnificent, spotted wings.

"Hello," Ms. Acara nodded at the creature. "Thank you for stopping by. Fiona here has never met a peryton. Hadn't even heard of one until I brought it up just now." Ms. Acara made a noise that was somewhere between a giggle and a hiccup. "Fiona, this is a peryton."

Fiona stood in awe. Though the Artificial Key was showing Fiona the peryton through a screen, the clarity and depth of the image felt as though the animal was right in front of her. She wished she could pat the peryton's soft head. "It's beautiful," she said.

The peryton blushed.

"Perytons are a sort of cross between a deer and a fairy," Ms. Acara said.

The peryton chirped and shook her head. Then she extended her wings and beat them powerfully. Fiona thought she could feel the air in the Sound Bubble being pushed around. It seemed like the peryton was saying that her wings were not dainty like fairy wings.

"Fine, not a fairy then. How about a cross between a deer and an eagle?"

The peryton bowed its head.

In the quiet of the Sound Bubble without Ferris around to hear, Fiona ventured a question. "Do you think Torien could ever make me an Artificial Key? I'm...," Fiona wasn't sure whether she could confide in Ms. Acara. In the end, she decided that if anything went wrong—if Ms. Acara laughed or called her names—she could walk away from this party and never see her again. She continued, "I'm afraid of losing my friend. He is from Fugue, and I'm not sure my parents will let me visit once he goes home."

"We haven't decided on distribution yet, but it is possible," Ms. Acara answered professionally. "I wouldn't get your hopes up though, Torien is a very busy man. People always want things from him, and it grows tiresome."

Fiona nodded. She hadn't expected a yes, but she had to ask.

"If I may be blunt—" Ms. Acara started. Her eyes floated down to Fiona's cheeks.

Fiona knew where the lawyer's train of thought was going. Her stomach sank. *Not now*, she thought.

"How did you get your makeup to look so natural? I love reds in my palette. Is that a new blend?"

Fiona touched her hand to her cheek. She felt the need to check whether she was actually wearing makeup. She wasn't of course. It was just that she'd never been asked about her skin in a way that was more admiring than disparaging. A surge of hope welled in her chest. Maybe it wasn't that she didn't fit in at home, maybe she just belonged somewhere else. "It's actually just my freckles," she said with a small smile.

Ms. Acara nodded slowly, not quite seeming to believe her. Then, before Fiona could stop her, Ms. Acara licked the tip of her thumb and stuck it against Fiona's cheek.

It was horrible. And wet. The hope expelled out of Fiona's chest like a popped balloon. She had to leave.

Chapter 10

Arti appeared next to the Sound Bubble and mimed a knocking motion. Ms. Acara swiftly tapped the screen to turn it off. The peryton disappeared from view and the noise of the room rushed in.

"Terribly sorry to interrupt," said Arti, "but dessert is ready. Would you care for a slice of fruit salad?"

Ms. Acara nodded emphatically. Arti pulled a silver remote from his suit. This one was smaller than the one that controlled his bike. It was no bigger than the buttons on Fiona's jacket. Arti zigzagged his thumb over the little silver joystick.

From across the room, the cake wiggled towards them, propped up by a set of eight spidery metal legs. Arti skillfully cut a paper-thin slice through each fruity layer of the cake and folded it like origami into a peryton. He handed the slice to Ms. Acara.

"Where's Ferris?" Fiona asked before Arti could offer her a slice of cake. "Did he talk to Torien yet? I want to leave."

Arti took a step back, surprised at Fiona's sudden change in mood. "I haven't seen him since he finished off the worm waffles. He's got to be around here somewhere."

"How do you know that? How do you know he hasn't rejected me like everyone else?"

Arti paused and blinked rapidly. "You think he left us? I knew I was getting on his nerves a bit, but to leave a party before dessert is served... well that just takes the cake, doesn't it?"

Fiona let out a breath of air. A smile crept across her face. Arti couldn't consider for even a second that Ferris would leave because of her. And he'd used a word only friends use. He'd said *us*. Fiona shook off whatever negative feelings still remained from her encounter with the patent lawyer. "Why don't you look downstairs, and I'll look upstairs? He's pretty small. We could have just missed him," Fiona suggested.

"Give him the benefit of the doubt. Yes, good idea, I like it!" Arti said, taking off towards the stairwell.

Fiona made her way to the kitchen. She knocked on the bathroom door. She wasn't sure if frogs used toilets. Maybe Ferris needed to splash some water over himself. He had been away from his foggy home for a while now. The bright Electronican sun was probably bad for his delicate skin. Not that Ferris would admit anything about him was delicate.

The bathroom was empty.

Fiona moved through the living room and into a hallway where a roaring fire raged on the wall's screen. She made a mental note never to visit whatever world that screen was showing. As she passed the fire wall, her shadow appeared on the screen. It was taller than she was. It moved slower than she did. And its hair wasn't curly. It was straight.

Fiona's insides turned icy. It wasn't her shadow. It was *the* shadow. The one she had seen in the woods before she knew the Great Piano existed. She recognized it by its fuzzy outline, the way part of itself seemed to stay behind as it moved. Fiona stood frozen as the shadow caught up to her. It turned and reached out its arms. She had a feeling it wasn't looking for a hug. Where were its hands?

Fiona ran. The fire wall spanned a long hallway. She ran as fast as she could through the strange house. She ran until she found a room without screens. She hoped the shadow couldn't get to her there. What was it doing in that fire world? Surely, no human could survive that. And if it wasn't human, what was it?

There was another question Fiona didn't even want to consider. The shadow had been outside her home. Now it was at Torien's house. Was it looking for her?

Fiona needed to find Ferris. They needed to get as far away from the Artificial Key as possible. It had seemed like the shadow wanted something from her. Her gut told her it wasn't friendship. She wasn't sure the shadow would stay in the fire world now that it had seen her.

Fiona scanned the area outside the chilly room she was in. She spotted the stairs. No screens lined the stairwell and she hadn't looked for Ferris up there yet. She hoped the coast was clear as she sprinted upstairs.

At the top of them was a round theater with glimmering gray walls and plush leather chairs. Ferris sat near the back of the room, taking up very little space in his seat. Fiona would've breathed a sigh of relief at seeing the frog, except that she was out of breath.

"Ferris," Fiona panted. "We need to—" then she noticed the glassy stare in Ferris's eyes. "Are you okay?"

"It's incredible, isn't it?" he replied in a far-off voice.

Fiona wasn't sure what Ferris was referring to. And her mind wasn't in the right place to think about it. "Sure," she agreed. "I've never been in a round theater before."

"Not the room Fiona. Fugue."

Fiona looked again at the gray walls and saw they were actually screens. The sparkle she had seen was fog. Every so often, a flash of color hopped across the screen, perhaps a friend of Ferris's, unaware they were being watched. Instinctively, Fiona backed away from the wall. But the shadow couldn't have made it to Fugue that quickly, could it? And if it was looking for her, it would be headed towards Electronica, not Fugue. She took a deep breath to shake off her nerves. "Ferris, I need to tell you someth—"

"—Louis is yellow and green, if you were wondering. Keep an eye out for him."

Fiona thought there were other things she should be keeping an eye out for, but Ferris had enough on his mind. "Did you try to start a conversation?"

"I can't. They don't know I'm here. They wouldn't know how to use the technology even if they did. We only have hardware in Fugue—head lamps, watches, radios. None of this computer stuff."

Fiona's mouth pulled to one side. "I'm sorry. I wish you could talk to them now. We'll be there soon though. We just need to get the key from Torien and then you'll be on this screen too."

"I hope you're right," Ferris said. "I keep looking for Louis. I want to know he's okay. I want him to know I'm okay. Can't imagine how I'd feel if he disappeared like I did."

"Splendid! You've found Ferris and the theater." Arti entered the room without noticing the sadness in it. He clicked his heels together, stood up straight and spoke in a formal tone to no one in particular. "I'd like to introduce you to an innovative young woman and her amphibious companion. This is Fiona—*what's your last name?*" Arti whispered.

"Duet," she whispered back, not sure who she was being introduced to.

"This is Fiona Duet and Ferris of Fugue," Arti concluded.

The screens flashed a bright blue, the kind of blue that means your computer is broken. It wasn't pleasant to stare at. Fiona tried to blink the glare away. When she opened her eyes, a floating head hovered on the screen.

"Mmhmm," said Torien Umba dismissively. Ferris jumped at the appearance of the man. Torien narrowed impatient brown eyes at Fiona. "I don't recall inviting you."

Fiona recognized his voice as the one that had greeted them in the kitchen.

Arti jumped in. "Yes sir, of course, but they were lost, and they helped me with the dessert."

"So you invited the help to my party?"

Arti opened his mouth to speak, but no words came out. He couldn't please everyone.

"Where are you?" Fiona asked boldly. It was odd someone would video call in to a party they were hosting.

Torien scoffed. "Are you blind? That would explain the dirt on your clothes."

Fiona examined her mostly-dry pants. There was some mud she hadn't managed to remove, but she didn't think it warranted the level of rudeness Torien was exhibiting.

"I'm in front of you is where I am." As Torien spoke, his head bounced away, so he wasn't actually in front of Fiona but beside her. He didn't seem able to hold himself still on the screen.

Fiona turned to follow him. "But you... couldn't be here in person at your party?"

Torien sighed discontentedly. "I can't be in person anywhere anymore. I'm dead."

She took a moment to process this. Maybe Torien had meant he was dead tired. Or dead funny. Maybe it was a slang Electronican term. He couldn't mean he was actually dead. "How do you have parties if you're dead?"

Torien glared at Fiona. He seemed to be hoping she might stop asking questions if he didn't answer them. Fiona stared back at the man. She was too curious not to get an answer. And Torien didn't know how patient she could be.

Seconds passed in silence. Torien gave in. "I knew death was coming for me," he began reluctantly. "I was sick for a long time. Before I passed, I uploaded my consciousness to the cloud. Now I live anywhere there is internet. I only come home to introduce a new technology of mine."

So Torien did mean dead. Dead dead. Ferris shifted uncomfortably in his seat. It was strange talking to a ghost.

Now that Torien was explaining himself, he seemed to enjoy the sound of his own voice. Fiona put on her best "I'm listening" face, and he continued. "I designed my house with screens for walls so when I have parties I can walk from room to room, float between conversations. It's just as good as real life," Torien said assuredly, but something in his eyes made that difficult for Fiona to believe. "My hologram is almost ready. I'll be able to walk without screens then. I'll be the first being to live completely in the cloud."

Not exactly, Fiona thought. She had seen someone living in a cloud on the way to Torien's house. Though, she supposed that was a different kind of cloud and nodded agreeably. If she was going to get Torien to answer her questions about Fugue, now was the time. "Mr. Umba, we're trying to get Ferris back home. Do you happen to have a key?"

Torien avoided her gaze. "I haven't a need for physical things anymore."

Fiona could see anguish in his eyes now. Maybe the only reason Torien was unhappy was because he spent most of his days alone, bobbing around a screen. Maybe the only time he wasn't lonely was at these parties. She could understand that.

He continued. "There aren't many keys that will get you to Fugue anyway. But I can tell you to look for a black key. White keys lead to worlds governed by humans. The sharps and flats, the black keys, lead to non-human worlds."

"Non-human?" asked Ferris.

"Animals, mythical beings, caricatures. Since Fugue is governed by frogs, you need a black key to get in."

"But how do we find the *right* black key?" asked Fiona.

"That's enough questions. I have other guests to see, you know." Torien grunted. "It should be obvious anyway. You'll know the key when you find it. It'll be—"

The internet cut out.

Torien froze. The screen shut off, leaving Fiona, Ferris, and Arti in the dark.

"I guess the party's over," joked Arti, trying to lighten the mood.

"No," said Ferris. He pounded his fist against the chair. "No that can't be it. Turn him back on!"

"I—There's nothing I can do, Ferris." Arti said meekly. "I'm a baker not a systems manager."

"I have to know…" Ferris trailed off. Unlike Torien, he didn't have to finish his sentence for Fiona to know what he was thinking. Was Louis safe? Did he miss Ferris? Where was the key and what was the fastest way home? The frog turned to Fiona. "Can we go?" he croaked.

Fiona picked Ferris up out of the chair. They now knew they were looking for a black key, but they still had no idea how or where to find the one to Fugue. Worse than that, if they found the wrong black key, what would be on the other side of those trees? Fiona envisioned an entire world of shadow people, but she couldn't let fear envelop her like it did the people in Arti's story. Besides, seeing Ferris this heartbroken made her more determined than ever. She couldn't leave Electronica until they had a key.

"Can we sleep in your cakery tonight?" she asked Arti. The shadow had seen her at Torien's house. If it was following her, it would go there. And the bakery had to be safer than wandering around the Fermata woods without a key.

"Abso-fruit-ly! I keep a cot there for my late-night bakes. Let me finish cleaning up and I'll take you back."

As the trio left Torien's house, Fiona felt like they were forgetting something. She might've been thinking of the cake they no longer had to carry. Or maybe it was the questions without answers tugging on her brain.

Outside, the roller skates were waiting to take them home. Ferris selected the setting *wander hopelessly*.

Chapter 11

When Fiona woke the next morning, it took her a moment to remember where she was. Ferris stirred on the pillow beside her. The cot in the bakery was not very comfortable. The metal support bar pressed into her back through the thin mattress. The room was cold and the blanket too thin, but Fiona had slept well despite this.

As she awoke, she thought about her parents. She usually woke to the sound of them shuffling about the house. They always had every intention of being quiet but somehow her mother banged every pot in the kitchen as she cooked. And she wasn't sure her father actually knew what a whisper was. Fiona hoped Arti was right about time passing differently within the trees or they'd be worried sick.

Still, it was nothing compared to what Ferris was going through. He didn't even know how long he'd been away from his husband. Fugue was probably littered with Missing Frog signs. A distraught Louis was probably out there painting rock homes the same shade of gray as the rock itself. Fiona squeezed her eyes shut and tried to send encouraging thoughts to Louis telepathically. It wouldn't work, but it was all she could do.

Ferris broke the silence in a groggy voice. "You know what I was thinking?"

"No," answered Fiona sleepily.

"Even though Torien never finished his sentence, he said finding the key will be obvious. He said we'll know when we've found the right one."

It was too early in the morning for Fiona to think straight.

"That means," Ferris persisted, "there must be something about the key that will tell us it's the one to Fugue."

Fiona considered this. "I wonder what that could be."

Ferris jumped, "I bet the key will give me a clue—the sound of it or the feel of it—I bet I'll recognize it somehow."

FIONA AND THE FORGOTTEN PIANO

Fiona nodded. "I bet you're right." She was particularly agreeable in the morning.

The sun shone brilliantly through the bakery window. The bell above the door tinkled. A tall, thin shadow crossed the bakery floor.

Fiona nearly launched herself out of bed. She wasn't a fighter, but she would do it to save herself if she had to. How does someone fight a shadow anyway? Did Electronica have shadow fighting lessons in school? Maybe instead of fighting she could hide behind the counter.

Arti's friendly voice interrupted Fiona's thoughts. The shadow belonged to him. "I can make you French toast if you like. I bet you two want to get on with your journey. Maybe a caterpillar omelet for Ferris?"

"No, we really ought to be going," Fiona replied, a little too quickly. She couldn't give the shadow more time to find her.

Ferris looked at Fiona like she'd gone mad. She hadn't told him about the shadow yet. The timing didn't feel right. He was so upset yesterday; she didn't want to add anything to his plate. "Fiona's joking." Ferris said. "I'll have ten caterpillar omelets."

Arti started to laugh but then seemed to think better of it. "Ten. Oh my. That will be a challenge."

"One I'm willing to take," Ferris replied.

Arti propped the bakery door open. Fiona realized her cot was taking up space for potential customers. She folded sheets as Arti retreated into the kitchen.

Ferris seemed like he was in a better mood, but the thought of telling him about the shadow still made Fiona uneasy. She was sure she was going to sound crazy. But with Arti out of the room, now was as good a time as any.

"Ferris, I don't know how to tell you this but..." She chewed on the inside of her cheek.

"I know, I snore."

"No, it's not that."

"Sleep talking then? Louis says I say weird things sometimes. I don't mean anything by them."

"No, it's not that either." Fiona glanced nervously out the shop window. With each person that passed, her stomach did a jumping jack. Maybe worries were like cakes, meant to be shared. "I think we're being followed," Fiona pulled on one of her curls. "Before I met you, I saw someone, some thing out in the woods. It wasn't quite a person, more like a shadow of one. And last night, at Torien's house, I saw it again."

Ferris cocked his head. "You saw someone twice. That doesn't seem worth worrying about. What makes you think they're following us?"

"I don't know. But strange things have been happening to me recently. At my piano recital, I knew how to play a song I'd never learned. And all of a sudden, I can recognize any note. Then I met you. I mean, not that you're strange. Maybe unusual is a better word." Ferris frowned. "No, not unusual. Anyway, you see my point. I've lived next to the Fermata woods my whole life. Why is it only now these things are happening? I think it has to do with the shadow."

"Hmm, maybe. But I still don't know what a shadow would want with a girl."

"I don't either. All I know is I get this really uneasy feeling when I see it, like it doesn't want me around."

Ferris sighed. "I see where this is going. You want to go home then? You know your way back," he said with a twinge of bitterness.

Fiona shook her head. "That's not what I want. I'm going to help get you home. We're... we're friends now. Plus I promised and I don't like breaking promises. We just have to keep an eye out is all."

"Oh." Ferris seemed surprised. "Right. If you think something is following us, we'll be careful. Move quickly. Not stay in any one place too long."

With the sentiment in mind, Ferris ate his ten omelets before Fiona finished even one slice of her French toast, which was not to say she didn't enjoy her breakfast. In fact, she hated to admit it, but she was glad her mom wasn't around to make leftover gummy cake omelets.

Seeing Ferris's empty plate, Arti beamed. "I wish I could've helped you two find your key, but I'll at least walk you to the tree portal. I just have to lock up." He grabbed his keys. Then he pulled the door stop out from under the door.

"Arti!" Ferris shouted.

Arti put a startled hand to his heart. It was the first time Ferris had spoken to him without mumbling since they'd met.

"The doorstop—it's a key!" Ferris said.

"Gravy, you're right. I can't believe I didn't notice it before." Arti examined the doorstop in his hand. "It's a little beat up, but you're welcome to take it. I don't even know where it goes."

The key was white, so it didn't have a chance of leading them to Fugue, but it might lead somewhere they'd have another chance at finding a black key. Fiona slipped it into her coat pocket.

The streets were quieter now. The layers of vehicles had thinned. Many of the commuters looked like they could've been Fiona's great grandparents, not because they bore any resemblance to Fiona but because she guessed they were about one hundred years old. The mechanical animals she'd seen yesterday were replaced by real horses and graceful floating sailboats. There was even a car or two, though they must've been electric because she didn't hear any engines.

Arti accompanied Fiona and Ferris on their walk to the tree portal. He managed to fill the quiet atmosphere with talk of how stretched out marshmallows would actually make really great sails.

"Come back anytime," he said when they reached the portal's silver gates. "I'll have grasshopper cake at the ready."

The words "Discovery Awaits" glittered in the sun. As inspiring a motto as it was, Fiona swallowed anxiously. She wasn't quite ready to leave. She didn't know what to expect in another world. She had a feeling they'd gotten lucky ending up in Electronica. "Can I ask one thing?"

Arti bowed in response.

"How come you never mentioned my spots? People usually feel the need to comment on them, but you didn't."

Arti nodded thoughtfully. "We all have our quirks, Fiona. You just happen to wear yours on the outside."

It was true, at least in Electronica; people had their quirks. It was different at home. No one wore snakeskin makeup there. Still, Fiona felt warmer with the encouragement. She waved goodbye and entered the tree portal with Ferris behind her.

$\oint \sharp \natural \, \flat \, \natural \, \sharp \, \natural \, \flat$

After a few steps of complete darkness, they were back in the woods. The moon greeted Fiona with its dim white light. It shone from the same place in the sky as before they'd entered Electronica. It was too perfect to be a coincidence. Arti must've been right about time zones. She hadn't missed a second in Songfield.

Though the moon's glow didn't cover every inch of the woods. Fiona found herself wondering, did shadows need light to exist? Or would nighttime be the perfect camouflage? She reached for her flashlight and clicked its button, but the light didn't turn on. She returned it to her pocket and gripped the new key. Ferris tracked her still fresh footprints back to the piano. There was unspoken agreement between them to move with haste.

Just as they had before, Fiona placed the key in the piano while Ferris hopped into the keybed and repaired it. Fiona decided this key was an F, a few octaves higher than the last key had been. She played the connected key, its note traveling in the opposite direction from which they'd come. She and Ferris chased after it. This time, she couldn't worry about tripping over roots. They had to enter the next world, somewhere the shadow couldn't find them.

At the end of the note was a birch tree. It had three thick branches like a fork. The tree grew a round, white doorknob in its trunk and a small door popped open without Fiona or Ferris having to open it. It was almost as if it had been waiting for them.

The door was smaller than the one that had led to Electronica. Fiona had to hunch to fit through it. In the darkness of the tree, the sound of her own rapid heartbeat filled her ears. She didn't know what to expect on the other side of the portal, she only knew what *not* to expect. She wouldn't find herself in Fugue or Electronica. It was unlikely this world would be as pleasant as Arti's French toast. She could only hope it wasn't a fiery nightmare.

Fiona's heartbeat was drowned out by the sound of waves crashing against a shore. The portal opened to a serene blue-gray sky. She allowed herself a deep breath. They were standing at the center of a clean, open beach. A chill ruffled Fiona's hair. Except for three seagulls flying overhead, they were alone.

Ferris slipped on the fine sand as he tried to crawl. When he realized he wasn't making forward progress, he dug frantically in it. "There's got to be a key here somewhere," he said, kicking coarse granules onto Fiona's ankles.

The sand wriggled its way into Fiona's shoes and scratched at her feet. Ferris was anxious. The salty sea air didn't seem to have the same calming effect on him that it had on Fiona. She needed to calm him down if they were going to find anything. "I went metal detecting with my grandfather once. We scanned the beach for hours, and after all that, do you know what we found?" Fiona took off one shoe at a time to rid them of sand. "A bottle cap and a dime. If there are any keys here, it's going to take forever to find them."

Ferris grumbled but stopped digging. "What do you suppose we do then?"

"We used a white key to get here which means this world is governed by humans. I say we find some of those humans and ask them where to find a black key."

"Hmph. You'll have to carry me. I can't walk on these tiny rocks."

Fiona extended an arm, and Ferris hopped on. She walked up the coast in the direction the seagulls had flown. Seagulls were usually more interested in French fries than fish. Maybe the smell of something fried was guiding their flight. And as far as she knew, only humans knew how to fry food.

Fiona trudged through the sand for what felt like miles without seeing another soul. Her calves ached. Her socks rubbed at her heels. She took a break to remove the scratchy socks and her bare feet softened in the sand. Finally, she came upon a large white tent with a pointed top.

A sign hung from tattered rope:

Card Readers of Chords

Past, Present &

Fiona read the sign twice. Someone must have forgotten to finish it. Surely it should have said "Past, Present & Future."

She hesitated at the door. Should she knock? Would the fabric make a sound if she did knock? Ferris was already pushing through it. He didn't really understand manners.

Chapter 12

It was humid inside. Fiona's hair puffed up and she tucked it behind her ear. The tent smelled of wool from the rugs layering the floor. The walls were covered in intricate fabrics. It was the kind of place Fiona could fall asleep in. Maybe Ferris could tuck her in under one of the wall hangings.

"We have visitors!" sang a woman. The edges of her long, pleated skirt hung over an ironing board. She had apparently felt the need to straighten the pleats but hadn't had time to change first.

"Wonderful," breathed another who was cozied up with a textbook. Fiona tilted her head to read its title: *Ancient History of Chordian Talent*. The book's spine had as many folds as were in the pleated skirt, as though had been read hundreds of times. "It's been sixteen hours since we last had visitors."

The two women had skin like sand and hair like sea glass, one green and one lavender. The lavender-haired woman offered Fiona and Ferris a seat on a lumpy floral couch. The green-haired woman offered them tea. The women introduced themselves as Mari and Rina.

The purple-haired Mari cleared her throat. "Are you ready for the show?" she asked.

"I didn't know there was—"

"Welcome..." said Rina with a twirl.

"To our..." said Mari with a kick.

They paused. Fiona wasn't sure what kind of performance this was. It wasn't quite good enough to be a dance. It wasn't exactly a song either. Perhaps it was an attempt at spoken word poetry.

"Have a seat." Rina gestured grandly to the couch Fiona was already sitting on.

"You look..." Mari touched Fiona's chin but once again didn't finish her sentence and Fiona was left wondering how she looked.

"Take some tea." Rina pulled four full teacups from behind her back, seemingly out of nowhere. Maybe this was a magic show.

"We're card readers, three!" Mari exclaimed, fanning herself with a deck of cards.

"Two!" Rina corrected.

"Two," Mari agreed.

"We're here if you'd just like to..." Rina curtsied. Mari curtsied after her. The show was seemingly over.

Fiona made confused eye contact with Ferris. He looked just as lost as she felt. "How come your sign only says 'Past, Present and?'" she blurted out.

Rina giggled and sipped her tea down in one gulp. "Clever, clever. We haven't been asked about that sign in six-hundred-eighty-five days." Rina pulled a folding chair from behind a fabric wall hanging and sat across from Fiona and Ferris.

Mari joined Rina on the same small seat. "We're triplets," Mari explained, wriggling her feet on the floor. "Our sister Vihuela is leaving Chords years ago. Something about love. Another world. She is leaving before travel is difficult." Mari elbowed her sister. "You finish the story. You know I can't speak in past tense."

Rina retaliated, bumping Mari off the chair with her hip. Mari huffed but didn't get off the floor.

"Like Mari said"—Rina sipped from her sister's teacup—"Vihuela left Chords just before the Piano Commission disbanded. We haven't seen her since."

Fiona didn't know what it was like to have siblings, but she understood how it felt to be homesick. She imagined missing a sibling was like that. People missed their sisters even if they bumped them off chairs. And she missed her mom even if she clung to an endless supply of rules.

"I know she wants to visit though. I can feel it." Mari said, looking towards the opening of the tent. Faith twinkled in her eyes. "To answer your question, I interpret the present. Rina reads the past."

"And Vihuela specialized in the future. It's been four thousand seven hundred twenty-six days since Vi left. No reason the sign should say 'future' anymore." Rina sighed.

Fiona sunk a bit deeper into the couch. She hoped Ferris's husband hadn't erased his name from anything yet. It didn't sound like the triplets had even tried to search for their sister. Fiona couldn't understand why. They didn't seem the type to fear traveling, not unless they cloaked their fears under silly antics and colorful fabrics. Maybe by the time they had gotten up the courage to look for Vihuela it had been too late. The keys had all been taken from the piano and they had nowhere to go. It wasn't right. A few people afraid of visitors shouldn't keep families apart.

Mari fiddled with her rings. "If you haven't noticed, everything in Chords comes in threes. It's difficult being a twosome here. Actually, you two should consider making a friend."

Fiona's eyes darted around the tent. Indeed, it had three sides. On each side were three wall hangings and below them, three rugs. "Does something bad happen if there are only two of you?"

"You'll feel a bit off balance. I often find myself walking like this..." Mari stood and circled the tent like she was wobbling on a tightrope.

"Do you feel off balance? Being just a girl and a frog?" Rina asked.

Fiona thought about it. Off balance wasn't really the right word. At times, she felt anxious, insecure, or out of place in these strange worlds, but that wasn't all that different from how she felt at home. At least here she could blame the rule of three for those feelings.

Before Fiona could answer, Mari jumped up and rubbed her hands together. She didn't appear able to sit still for very long. For someone who specialized in the present, she didn't seem at peace in it. Maybe specializing in the present meant you could never really *be* present. Mari seemed to be everywhere all at once all the time. "Let me get my cards while you think of the real question you want to ask us," she said.

Rina stood and pulled a folding table from behind another piece of fabric. How much furniture were they storing back there? Was there anything under the rugs? Fiona slid a toe beneath the rug at her feet and flipped up the corner of it. A single card stuck to the floor. She held in a giggle.

Rina unfolded the table and positioned herself across from the couch. She leaned onto her elbows and tilted her head, gazing at Fiona with great interest. It made Fiona slightly uncomfortable. She didn't know whether she was supposed to look around the room or if it was more polite to make intense eye contact back. She tried the eye contact thing. After a few moments, her eyes shifted awkwardly away all on their own.

"Have you ever had your freckles looked at?" Rina asked. Fiona should've expected the question. For some reason, she hadn't even thought about her spots when she entered the tent and Rina's question didn't sting as much as it normally would. There was no malice or judgment behind it, only unfiltered curiosity.

"The doctor said not to worry about them if they aren't bothering me," Fiona said.

The woman raised an eyebrow. "I didn't mean looked at by a doctor. Freckles can be interpreted like tea leaves. It's not my specialty but yours are honestly extraordinary."

Extraordinary was one of Fiona's spelling words last year. It meant strange and wonderful. The word sat well with her, warming her like steaming hot broth on a cold day. Or perhaps like the green tea Rina was now pouring herself another cup of. Her freckles were definitely strange, but maybe they were wonderful too.

Ferris grumbled to himself, impatience winning out over his other emotions. He whispered to Fiona, "It's just our luck, it's the future sister who left—the one we need most!"

"I wouldn't be so sure of that," said Mari, who apparently had very good hearing. She pulled a deck of cards from the bottom drawer of a bureau on the other side of the tent. "Your past and present can tell you more than you think," she said, making her way back to the folding table.

Rina unpinned a starry fabric from the wall and covered the folding table with it. "Have you thought of your question?"

Fiona hadn't thought about it. She didn't have to. It was the same question that had been on her mind since she'd learned where Ferris was truly from. "We'd like to know how to get Ferris home."

Mari laid the cards on the table. Rina shuffled them behind her back and fanned them out. "Choose three."

Fiona slid the first card out of the deck. Ferris flicked his tongue out to select the second. Rina's mouth turned down in disgust. Mari's eyes widened in amusement. For the third card, Fiona reached under the rug and picked up the card she'd found earlier.

"You do magic?" Rina asked with surprise.

"Oh no, I just saw the card there before," Fiona said.

"It looked like magic." Rina's amazement at Fiona's ability to pick a card off the floor made Fiona question how much she could trust this reading. Well, more than she already was questioning it.

"Isn't that fortuitous? Found cards give better readings than picked ones." Mari rejoined Rina on the folding chair and flipped over the three cards. The first showed a family of three picnicking beneath a rainbow.

"The first card represents the past," Rina put her finger in the center of the rainbow. "This is the Six of Strings. It's in reverse, which is unfortunate. In the upright position, this card would symbolize happiness and fulfilled dreams. In the reverse, it signifies heartbreak and tension in the family."

Fiona leaned in to get a better look at the card. From where she was sitting, the rainbow *was* in the upright position. And she certainly felt more like she was on a path to fulfilled dreams than heartbreak. Sure, none of the Great

Piano's worlds were perfect, but if people could accept her spots, that was as close to content as she'd been in a long time.

"Did your parents separate? Do you have other siblings? Were you supposed to?" Rina's questions buzzed around the tent.

Fiona wanted to bat them down. She shook her head, more in disbelief than as an answer. As far as she knew, her parents were happy, and her father always said he only wanted one kid to spoil. The green-haired woman couldn't really know anything about her family anyway. The reading seemed more relevant for Ferris. He was separated from his husband. Actually, even Rina herself was a better candidate for the reading. She was missing a sister, and the card was upside-down from her point of view. Fiona closed her eyes. Her family was fine. The card was wrong.

Mari sensed Fiona's discomfort at the reading. "Try not to stress too much about it. Whatever it is, it's in the past."

"No," countered Rina in a sing-song voice. "It *started* in the past, but it's still a part of her family's life now."

Fiona's jaw tightened as she shoved anxious thoughts from her head.

Mari shot Rina a look that said, 'stop scaring the girl' and continued to the second card. On its face, an old man stood on a cliff. He held a lantern in his outstretched hand. The man had slender limbs and a round belly. It was how Fiona imagined Ferris would look as a human, except Ferris would use a headlamp. Fiona's jaw loosened. At least this card wouldn't be about her. "This is the Nine of Melodies. You can see there are nine stars in the sky above the old man. This card will lead you to the black key you seek."

Ferris put a webbed foot on Fiona's finger. They hadn't mentioned the key to the sisters.

"Knowing the present is more important than you think," said Mari, pulling at her sleeves. "At any given moment, I can sense where something is. I don't know where it came from or where it's going, but sometimes where it *is* is all that matters."

Ferris leaned forward, as if getting closer to Mari would reveal the answer sooner.

Mari twirled her hair in her fingers. "The black key you seek is in Chords, but it is not nearby. Presently, you are in Major Chords. You'll only find white keys here. To reach the black key you seek, you must go to Minor Chords. There you will find a geyser that spews yellow smoke. That's where the black key is."

Rina grimaced.

Was there something wrong with Minor Chords?

"How do we get there?" asked Ferris anxiously.

"I don't know," answered Mari with an exaggerated shrug. "That is in the future, but it's best you don't dawdle. If the key moves, I won't be able to tell you where it has gone."

Ferris harrumphed.

"And the third card? What does that one mean?" asked Fiona. "Can it help us find our way?"

The third card was black and white. It displayed a man riding a chariot driven by a wild dog and a fearless cat. Rina put her hand over the card and closed her eyes in concentration. She pressed her lips together, willing a vision to come to her. Her voice dropped an octave. "Beware the Meadow Gnomes," she warned.

There was silence as Fiona and Ferris contemplated their fate with the Meadow Gnomes. Then Mari spit out a full-bellied laugh. "Meadow gnomes?" she mocked.

"You try then!" Rina crossed her arms.

"Our sincerest apologies. We really need Vi to read the final card, but I'll give it a go." Just as Rina had, Mari closed her eyes and pursed her lips. The resemblance between them was clear now. She began slowly. "You must avoid DC. I'm not sure which DC. Isn't there a Washington where you're from? Washington DC, maybe? Have you thought about going there?"

Fiona shook her head. So much for found cards giving better readings.

"There's definitely something with a D and a C," Mari said, biting her cheek.

Fiona looked at the dog and the cat on the card and wondered if she could have made the same prediction herself.

"That's the best you got?" teased Rina, nudging her sister.

"You're right. Seems unlikely," conceded Mari. She fidgeted with her bracelet.

What if the card had nothing to do with the letters D and C and everything to do with its lack of color? Fiona's stomach churned. Shadows don't have color. Maybe she hadn't escaped its path.

"More tea?" offered Rina. Rina's hair must've been green from drinking as much tea as she did.

"No, it's not," Mari answered the question Fiona hadn't asked out loud. "Our hair is a reflection of our talents. Chordians with minty locks can read the past. Those with mauve hair like me see the present."

"What color hair did your sister have?" Fiona asked.

Rina smiled at the memory of her sister. "It was a gorgeous Prussian blue. The same color as Ferris's legs."

Fiona touched her curls. If only they could take the red from her freckles. Red hair and dark freckles made more sense. No one would think twice if she looked like that.

Ferris tapped his fingers loudly on the table. He was growing impatient. "I don't know what you're talking about." Ferris hadn't heard the question Fiona asked in her head. He couldn't understand why the sisters were suddenly talking about hair color. "But like you said, we can't dawdle if we want to find the key at the yellow geyser."

"Naturally," Mari nodded. "But you must stay for the closing show."

"I don't think so," said Ferris, jumping off the couch.

"We'll do it very fast," said Rina, leaning over the table to finish the tea Ferris clearly wasn't going to drink.

"Have to go..." Ferris muttered heading for the door.

Mari jumped on the couch beside Fiona. Rina stood on the chair. The sisters spoke loudly but in harmony.

"You've had your reading...

It's time to...

There's one more thing...

Waves like the ocean...

We can't wait to have..."

It wasn't a very satisfying end to the poem, but that was where the sisters stopped. Fiona wasn't sure whether she was supposed to clap. "Th-thank you," she said, hoping that would satisfy them.

They gave big toothy smiles like they were waiting for something. A tip, maybe? But Fiona didn't have anything to give them. She rose slowly from the couch, lifted her hand in a wave and hurried out of the tent.

Chapter 13

Ferris jumped on a sand dune to survey their surroundings. The dune wasn't very tall, so he climbed to the top of a blade of beach grass. When he reached the tip of the blade, it curled over with the weight of him, and he found himself back on the sand.

"Pick me up," he demanded.

Fiona was still doing mental gymnastics to figure out what had happened in the card readers tent. There was a lot to digest. *Is something wrong with my family?* She picked up the frog absent-mindedly.

"Raise me above your head," Ferris instructed, and so Fiona did.

Am I destined to see the shadow again? Maybe she should've asked the sisters this question. But then she probably would've ended up with an answer as vague as "something about DC".

From Ferris's new height, he scanned the horizon. He pointed to the outline of a snowcapped volcano. "Alright, put me down," he said. "What we're going to do is walk with your right shoulder facing the sun. By midday, we should be close enough to that volcano to see geysers."

Fiona didn't even stop to question why Ferris thought there would be geysers near the volcano. She did pause at the mention of approaching a geologic feature filled with lava. "What are the chances it erupts?"

"Very low," Ferris said assuredly. "Most volcanoes are inactive for thousands of years at a time."

A nagging feeling tugged at the back of Fiona's mind. Something wasn't right about the volcano. But what other option did she have? She pulled at the sleeves of her coat. The only way to get the key was to head toward the mountainous gaping hole in the earth.

As Fiona and Ferris walked down the beach, the sand beneath their feet turned from tan to black. It became rough and gravelly, crunching under their footsteps. They could no longer see Rina and Mari's tent. Ferris complained of blistering feet and took his usual spot on Fiona's shoulder.

Fiona's mind was a carousel of questions. Over and over again they circled, taunting her like school children. She needed to focus. Find the key. Get Ferris home. She could sort out the other stuff later. "Sun to the right, ocean to the left," Fiona mumbled to herself. She hoped speaking aloud would break the cycle of dancing questions. *Is my family okay? Am I being followed?* The questions were still there. She repeated the directions again, louder this time. "Sun to the right, ocean to the left,"

"Do we have to shout?" Ferris asked.

Fiona hadn't taken into account how close Ferris's ears were to her mouth. "Sorry," she whispered.

She walked a bit further when Ferris sang out, "Sun to the right, ocean to the left." He had a surprisingly good voice.

"How come you're allowed to say it?" Fiona laughed.

"I can't help it. It's catchy."

"I think we spent too much time in that tent. The humidity got to your head," she teased.

"The humidity got to your hair," the frog retorted.

Fiona guffawed. She put a hand to the top of her head. Her fingers grazed her hair a good few inches above where they normally would.

"Too far?" Ferris chuckled.

Fiona stopped short. Too far was right, but not about the joke. The beach was quiet. The sound of crashing waves that had accompanied them on their journey had stopped. Why did the ocean go as quiet as the woods? Was it a Sound Bubble? Fiona moved to the shore to examine the seawater. Its waves were frozen. The ocean had turned to ice. She didn't even know oceans could do that.

"No bridge," Ferris said.

"Bridge?" Fiona didn't expect there would be a bridge to cross the ocean. She turned back to the path they'd been on and saw what Ferris was referring to. A crack in the earth, wide and deep, ran between the land dividing Major and Minor Chords. There was no sign to tell Fiona this, but she now understood why Rina had grimaced at the mention of Minor Chords. Frozen oceans, open crevices, volcanoes. She wasn't exactly excited to visit.

Fiona peered into the crevice. She couldn't see where it ended—if it ended. She bit her lip, evaluating their options. They couldn't turn back, not when the geyser was up ahead. They couldn't very well jump over the crack. It was too wide. If they tried, they'd certainly fall to their— well, better not to think about that too much. There was really only one choice. "We have to cross the ocean," she said, glancing at the uneven icy surface which flowed over the dividing crevice.

"Hope the ice is thick enough," Ferris gulped.

"Me too," Fiona nodded.

Ferris watched from the shore as Fiona tested the ice. It would certainly hold under the weight of a frog, but an eleven-year-old was a different story. If Fiona fell through, Ferris could leap back to the triplets' tent for help. She leaned onto the ice with one foot. It felt solid. It didn't move or crack. She tested the other foot.

"Try to distribute your weight," the frog advised.

Fiona shuffled forward, keeping her feet flat on the ice like she was skating, though she'd never been very good at skating. She swayed like a Jack-in-the-box, her upper body wobbling while her legs were stiff as tree trunks. "Seems stable to me," she called, her torso lurching forward.

"That's not very convincing," Ferris said. He crawled to meet her, though, so he must've at least been somewhat convinced.

The fissure between Major and Minor Chords was as wide as a house. In the distance, the top of the volcano was clear, but there were still miles between them and the towering mountain.

Fiona's wobbles moved to her legs. She was less Jack-in-the-box and more baby deer learning to walk. But could baby deer walk backwards? She spun and shuffle-slid back a few steps.

"Fiona." Ferris stopped in his tracks, tired of her antics probably. "Do you hear that?"

Fiona shifted her focus from her feet to her ears and listened. "I don't hear anything."

"It sounds like someone crying," said Ferris. He rested his head against the ice.

Fiona lowered onto all fours and turned her ear downwards. She heard nothing.

And then she did.

With a great pop, the ice broke open beneath her. Her stomach dropped as she fell through a hole in the ocean's surface.

Somehow she wasn't underwater. Fiona found herself sliding down a tunnel, her hair whipping around her head. Her legs chilled against the icy slide. Down and down she slid until the tunnel leveled off. It opened into a larger cave. Fiona rolled forward with the momentum of her descent.

Her hands trembled as the shock of the cold and the fall sunk in. She wasn't sure how far she'd fallen. It felt like at least four playground slides long. She pressed her hands into the floor around her. It seemed sturdy, but she'd thought that about the ocean's surface too. It was hard to situate herself. She might've been at the bottom of the ocean, or she might've been in the middle of it. Was that more or less safe than the surface? The frozen water surrounding her glowed sapphire. Icicles hung from the roof of the cave in dutiful groups of three. They threatened to crush her at any moment. It was beautiful and terrifying all at once.

As far as she knew, Ferris was still on the ocean's surface above. She positioned her head up through the tunnel. "Ferris?" she called. Her voice echoed. A shiver ran down her spine. She waited for a response, got none, and tried again. "Ferris, I'm safe! Slide down the tunnel and I'll catch you at the bottom."

"You expect me to jump through a hole in the ocean?" came the reply from above.

At hearing Ferris's voice, relief crashed through her. "Think of it as a shortcut. I see some light at the end of this cave. I bet it leads to Minor Chords."

A distinct groan echoed from above. Fiona took it to mean, 'I'll come down, but I am not happy about it.'

Frogs, as it turned out, were not made for sliding. Ferris had to tuck his sticky hands and feet close to his body in order to slide down the tunnel. This had the unfortunate effect of causing Ferris to swing up and down the sides of the ice like a pendulum in a clock. He twisted and turned. At one point, though it was certainly not his intention,

Ferris found himself sliding backwards and headfirst. He did a full three-hundred-and-sixty-degree rotation around the tunnel before he was thrown into Fiona's arms.

"Well," Ferris said, letting out a breath he'd been holding, "that was horrible."

Someone giggled.

"Don't laugh at me," said Ferris.

"I didn't," said Fiona, suddenly very aware of her heartbeat.

A hollow knock echoed in the cave. Fiona instinctively looked for a door, but of course there wasn't one. She backed into a corner, hoping if no one answered the knock, whatever it was would be on its merry way. *Tun tun tun*, the sound came again. Fiona swallowed. There was nowhere to run if the shadow was here.

Then she saw it. On the floor of the cave, trapped in a pocket of water under the ice, was an adorable amphibian. It was small like a gecko, colorful like a chameleon and sleek like a salamander. The little creature had cantaloupe skin and a pink feathery crown like seaweed. It had round, amber eyes and the smallest comforting smile. The creature wagged its tail and waved to Fiona. She bent to get a closer look.

Ferris inspected the cage of ice where the creature was swimming. "Lovely to meet you," he said. "We ought to be on our way now."

Fiona ignored him. "Do you need help?"

The amphibian nodded its head emphatically. Fiona took the flashlight from her pocket. She banged on the ice with the back end of it, smashing the flashlight in a circle around the frozen cage. Bit by bit, the ice chipped away. The creature pushed its feet against the cage from the other side until it cracked all the way through. Fiona slipped her fingers around the edges of the ice block and pulled the loosened chunk out, freeing the animal. The amphibian hopped out of the water, shook itself off and crawled up Fiona's arm, making itself at home on her dry shoulder.

"What's your name?" Fiona asked.

The creature smiled back at her.

"She doesn't have one," said Ferris.

"How do you know?" Fiona dragged a finger over the creature's head. Her skin was softer than Ferris's. Her demeanor was softer too.

"She told me."

"I didn't hear anything."

Ferris shrugged. "Her voice must be too high pitched for you."

Fiona frowned. The creature had to have a name. "Do you know what kind of animal she is?"

"She's an axolotl. They're like frogs that never grow out of their tadpole phase. She's unusual though. Those things on the top of her head are gills. They can't live outside of water, except this one apparently."

The axolotl wiggled her gills proudly and gulped the air to show she could breathe just fine.

"Gilly is a cute name," Fiona tried.

"Might as well name her Leggy," Ferris said.

"What?" Fiona didn't usually judge other people for their naming preferences but Leggy was particularly strange.

"If you're naming her after body parts."

"Oh." She should've known Ferris was being sarcastic. "What about Coral?"

The axolotl scrunched up her nose.

"That would be a no," Ferris clarified, though he didn't have to.

"Nori?" Fiona asked.

"*Wheeek*," the creature responded in a tone Fiona could hear but couldn't understand. The amphibian bounced happily. That was a yes then. She decided not to tell the animal nori is a seaweed people eat.

"We're on our way to find a black key in a yellow geyser," Fiona explained. "You're welcome to join us." Nori brushed her head up against Fiona's shoulder. She was probably happy to be anywhere that wasn't an ice cage.

The three of them made their way cautiously through the cave, avoiding the icicles. Ferris muttered to himself. He might've been jealous Nori got to sit on Fiona's shoulder while he was stuck walking. But since he didn't ask if he could sit on Fiona's other shoulder, he was stuck making grumpy noises on the ground.

Fiona had a sudden realization. "Ferris, I never thought to ask. Did you have a name before we met?"

"Of course, I have a name, but you wouldn't be able to pronounce it," Ferris said a bit bitterly.

An arrow of guilt shot Fiona in the chest. She'd taken Ferris from his home and taken his name. No wonder he was bitter. "I'd still like to know it."

"My name is *Errrut*," Ferris chirped, making a sound like a squeaky eraser.

"*Errrut*," Nori imitated perfectly.

"Anyway, Ferris suits me."

The arrow of guilt dissolved. Fiona's mouth lifted at the corners. At least he liked the name. "Is your husband's name really Louis?"

Ferris tilted his head. "Close enough. It's more like a high-pitched Louis with a silent L."

A bright spot shone where the cave opened. The light intensified as they marched closer to it. The sun on the other side warmed the cave's edges. Water droplets fell like rain.

The cave was melting.

Chapter 14

Fiona picked up her pace, though not as much as she wanted to. It was hard to move over the slippery floor, and she still didn't know if the ice beneath her would give way again. Ferris's feet were covered in a layer of icy slush that was accumulating too quickly for comfort.

Fiona's foot shot out behind her. She instinctively reached out to catch herself, grabbing onto a frosty icicle. It broke as soon as she got hold of it. Nori gripped the shoulder of Fiona's coat. Fiona's other foot lost its grip too, sending her body to the floor. She landed flat on her stomach, the air in her lungs escaped into the cave. She took short, deep breaths to try to get it back but the shock of the cold floor against her body only added to her breathing troubles.

After a moment, air crawled back into her lungs. Cold stuck to Fiona's body as water sunk into her pajamas. Her eyes watered. Her chin quivered. How many times would she fall before she succeeded? Why did no one ever offer to help?

As if in answer, Ferris called out. "Use the icicle as a walking stick. Remember what we did on the surface. Take small steps."

"I fell through the surface!" Fiona tried to steady her trembling chin. She didn't want to cry in front of Ferris.

"We're almost there. I promise. We're almost there. We can make it." He reassured her.

There was that comforting word. Fiona liked being part of a "we." If she could focus on the feeling it gave her, she could almost imagine she was back sipping tea in the card reader's tent. The frog's words were genuine. Maybe he did care. Maybe they were actually friends. She took a deep breath and stood, brushing off the ache in her ribs. She looked to the cave's opening. She would make it to the yellow geyser. She would find the key to Fugue.

When the trio reached the mouth of the cave, a flat, rocky surface stretched before them. The cracked, sun-baked rocks gave way to a looming volcano. Just one.

At the edge of view, hardy aspen trees endured. Their tattered leaves and thin trunks had turned orange with heat. There were no geysers in sight. Fiona swallowed. They couldn't have come all this way to not find a geyser. Ferris didn't appear concerned. At least someone was confident they were in the right spot.

The persistent sun dried Fiona's clothes. She took off her jacket and wrapped it around her waist, preparing for whatever came next. The warmth seemed to charge her skin and her mind. She was more determined than ever to get her friend home, no matter what she had to face.

Nori laid on a rock and rolled onto her back, soaking up the golden rays. Ferris appeared unaffected by the change of atmosphere. He might've actually been tired of sunlight. It only served as a reminder he was far from home. He turned his ear to the rocky surface. "We're close," Ferris said, sensing something Fiona couldn't feel.

From somewhere underground, a high-pitched whine like a tea kettle rang out. The note was an F sharp. And it was a warning. Three explosions of steam burst from the cracks between rocks. Nori jerked back to her feet.

Green, white, burgundy.

Fiona watched in awe as clouds of colorful water grew, mingled, and faded. The steam dissipated. But soon after, with a whistle, another three geysers erupted.

Black, orange, teal.

The accompanying note was a G sharp.

F sharp, G sharp.

Fiona felt something like a lock click at the back of her mind. She knew where this was going. After G sharp was—

The next set of geysers sang an A sharp before Fiona could finish her thought. The lock in her mind burst open. Fiona's eyes widened at the realization. The geysers were playing scales. Her fingers twitched as she moved them over an invisible piano.

Geysers continued around them like brush strokes in a painting, each one blending into the next, always in sets of three. Steam landed gracefully on Fiona's cheeks. Did Ferris feel at home among the geysers? He'd said his husband's art was his beacon home on gloomy nights. In a way, these geysers were a beacon home too.

But one glance at the frog told her he was too anxious to admire the geysers. He was busy scanning the horizon, his eyes darting left and right. He refused to miss a single burst of color. Where was the yellow one?

Another whistle, this time a D sharp.

Purple, brown, crimson.

Among the crimson steam, a speck of black flew into the air. It landed on the ground with a clank— a key.

"I'll get it!" Fiona exclaimed as she took off towards the crimson geyser. Nori bounded after her.

"It wasn't yellow," Ferris called back. But Fiona was already leaping to retrieve it. She ran through the maze of mist, hurdling over gaps in the rocky surface. After the sand and ice, it felt good to be on solid ground. It was like a game. The exploding geysers were defenders to be avoided.

The key had landed in a small divot, shielded from sunlight. Fiona picked it up. It was still damp and warm from the geyser's spray. She raced back to Ferris and placed it in front of him, hoping it would reveal itself as the right one. "What do you think? Is this it?"

Ferris touched the key. He put his ear to it. He shook it. Finally, he shrugged, doubt plain on his face. "There's nothing special about this one."

Fiona examined the piano key herself. She would hold onto it, just in case. She reached to place the key in what she believed was her lower left pocket, though the jacket around her waist was twisted at an odd angle from her sprint.

Pink, Cream, Navy.

Three more geysers shot off. They were different from the others. They didn't play the F note Fiona was expecting. Her heart sank. Ms. Downey had trained her to fear erroneous scales. One slip of her fingers on the keyboard resulted in a scolding. But her piano teacher wasn't here. So why was she afraid now?

CRACK.

POP.

BOOM.

The fireworks sound hadn't come from the geysers. It wasn't the warning whistle. It wasn't part of the scales. This was something bigger. A forceful vibration swam up Fiona's feet and into her chest. Nori squealed and pointed at the volcano. A heavy cloud of smoke billowed out of it.

"That can't be good," said Fiona, finally realizing why she'd felt uneasy about the volcano. The triplets had said everything in Chords came in threes. If things that came in twos were off balance, singular objects must be even worse. The volcano was alone, and it was going to erupt.

"We can't leave yet," said Ferris in a panic. "We haven't found the yellow geyser."

An impenetrable cloud of volcanic smoke spread across the sky, blocking out more and more sunlight as it expanded. "We don't have much longer," Fiona said. Was waiting for the geyser even worth it? They could find the key to Fugue another way. Anything had to be better than getting swallowed by molten rock.

"One more set of geysers. Please," Ferris pleaded.

Ferris wasn't usually one to beg. But he was right. If they didn't find the key now, there might not be another chance. "Okay," Fiona said. She was either very brave or very stupid. It wouldn't be long before she found out which.

Could she outrun lava if it came to that? She scanned their surroundings. If they couldn't leave, she could at least plan their escape. They couldn't go back the way they came. The melting tunnel leaked pools of water. There was no way they could climb back up it.

For now, the wall of ice surrounding the tunnel held. They could run along it towards the treeline. Once they were out of the valley, the aspen forest might rise high enough to meet the ocean's surface. If it was still frozen, they could cross back to Major Chords. If it wasn't, Fiona knew how to swim. She hoped the volcano's wrath wouldn't reach that far. It wasn't a perfect plan, but it was the best her racing mind could do.

The sky turned from gray to black as the ash continued to billow and spread. With a hiss as loud as a steamboat, three yellow geysers burst from the rock. They illuminated the black key that shot out of them. It flew straight into the sky and took its time on the way down. Floating back and forth like a feather until it landed neatly next to Ferris, spraying him gently with water droplets as it hit the ground.

Ferris wrapped an arm around the key. Fiona knew what he was thinking. The key could've landed anywhere, but it found Ferris. It chose him. It had to be the one to Fugue. Maybe that's what Torien had meant before he was hit by the internet's freeze ray. It wasn't that they'd know the key when they found it. Maybe it was that the key would find them. Ferris tried hoisting the piano key onto his back, not wanting to let it go. But he couldn't carry it and run, not efficiently anyway. Gripping the key with both hands, he raised it in the air for Fiona to take. "Keep this one safe," he said.

Fiona tucked the key away in the upper left pocket of her jacket. She snapped the pocket closed to secure it. The trio took off running toward the aspen trees. Neon lava as thick as clay bubbled as it rolled down the volcano. It snaked through crevices in the rock. They ran faster.

At the tree line, Nori tugged on Fiona's pant leg, urging her toward the volcano. Ferris continued towards the ocean. Fiona stopped. "Nori, we have to go. What is it?"

Nori squealed and tugged harder at her pants. Fiona hesitated, unsure whether to listen to the amphibian she'd just met or to follow the one who couldn't possibly know the way out. "Ferris," she called, "Can you translate for me?"

"There's no time! Let's get out of here!" he yelled back.

"I—I think it's important," Fiona insisted.

Ferris stomped his feet before giving in. He leapt back to Fiona. When he reached her, Nori chittered and pawed at the ground in explanation. Ferris's mouth popped open. "Follow the axolotl!" he said.

Nori grinned and took off into the forest, weaving in and out of heat-stricken trees. Fiona struggled to keep up. She didn't know where they were going, but she couldn't waste time asking questions. The lava at the base of the volcano crept over the rocks toward the trees. It snuffed out a blue geyser. If Ferris trusted Nori, she would too.

Nori paused at a tree with mahogany leaves. Holes covered its trunk and branches like insects had burrowed into it. It was on the verge of collapse. Nori climbed up the tree's brittle trunk and popped her head in and out of each hole. She was searching for something.

"*Cheeep*," the axolotl let out an animated squeak as she popped out of a hole in one of the tree's branches. She leapt from the branch to the leaf-covered ground.

The holes at the base of the tree began to grow. They grew to the size of baseballs. Ferris and Nori pushed on the bits of bark between the holes. Fiona joined in, though she hadn't a clue what she was doing. Pieces of bark cracked one by one until, with a final snap, a door opened. It was only as high as Fiona's knees. Where did it lead?

It dawned on her—this was Minor Chords. She and Ferris had entered this world through Major Chords. They didn't need to exit the same way they'd come. Nori fled through the doorway, leaving Fiona and Ferris on the other side.

"You go first," said Ferris. "It's a small door. We have to make sure you can get through."

Fiona got on her stomach. The ground was warm. She wanted to close her eyes, to imagine she was wrapped in a blanket in her bedroom. It was easier to believe none of this was real. But she forced her eyes open. She avoided turning her head in the direction of the lava that was surely parading towards them. She'd be swallowed by it if she didn't move. She pulled herself through the doorway on her forearms. Inside the tree, splinters clawed at her back. They scratched at her arms. If she'd have been twelve, she wouldn't have fit. She grimaced as she inched her way through the tree. She couldn't pause at the pain. Ferris had to make it through the portal too. She had to reach the other side. Now.

Chapter 15

Panic set in. What if the portal was still open when the lava hit the aspen tree? Would the Fermata woods flood with the burning rock? Would she be responsible for destroying all the Great Piano's portals? *Hurry up.*

Fiona's cheeks, red from heat and activity, were met with crisp soothing air. The world was quiet. There were no more whistles. No more scales or explosions. She shuddered to think how close she'd come to never seeing the woods again.

Ferris appeared in the doorway, gasping for clean air. He crawled to Fiona's knee and leaned on her leg. With a reassuring crackling sound, the tree's door sealed shut. No hot orange goo leaked out of it. They sat on the forest floor catching their breath. If it weren't for Nori, Fiona and Ferris might have been lost to Chords forever. The rule of three was right.

The axolotl rolled over, bathing in the cool soil of the woods. Fiona's mouth tipped up at the corners, glad to see their little protector was sticking around.

When their lungs recovered, Ferris stretched his legs. He and Fiona ambled through the woods back to the Great Piano. Nori was heading there too, but she was only following the girl and the frog, so she didn't know it.

"How does it feel to be so close to home?" Fiona asked.

Ferris seemed to have forgotten he was moments away from reentering Fugue because, at the reminder, he suddenly walked as if he had four springs installed where his legs had been. Nori must've asked something then because instead of answering Fiona's question, a downright joyful Ferris launched into an explanation of how the Great Piano worked. He told Nori about Electronica and Fugue. He even mentioned the time he spent in the tank in Fiona's room. "Heat lamps are marvelous things," he bragged. It warmed Fiona to hear Ferris speak of her world on the same level as the others. She had tried to make it comfortable for him.

When the trio reached the instrument, Fiona unsnapped her pocket and pulled out the black key. Ferris climbed into the piano with Nori and showed her how to repair it.

"It is a tight squeeze, but it's roomier than a pickle jar," Ferris chuckled. He was never going to let that go apparently.

"It was all I had," Fiona said in the direction of the fall board.

Nori giggled. Her cheer was contagious. If Rina and Mari's hair color reflected their talents, Nori's pink gills seemed to hold the gift of friendship.

Fiona pressed her ring finger down on the newly attached key. It tinged disappointingly. The note was weak and high-pitched.

From somewhere behind her, a branch snapped. Fiona froze. The amphibians were still in the piano. It was the middle of the night. Who else would be in the woods? *Please be a raccoon.* Even a rabid one would do. A bear! A bear would be better than the shadow. Fiona gulped. She turned in the direction of the sound. Only darkness lay before her.

A shuffling of leaves, closer this time. Close enough that whatever was making the sound should've been visible in the moonlight.

Ferris popped out of the keybed with Nori. "It's not what I expected. Somehow, I th—"

Fiona scooped the frog and the axolotl into her hands. She pressed the new key forcefully and chased after its note.

"What are y—"

"*Shhh*," Fiona cut Ferris off. He squirmed in her palm.

Fiona used everything she'd learned about navigating the woods in the dark. Her eyes adjusted to the low light. She gazed ahead, keeping a safe distance between the trees and their obstructive roots. She trusted her feet to catch her if they landed on uneven ground. She didn't dare look back.

She trusted her ears too. She could recognize any note, follow it to its source. This one was no different. The tree portal couldn't be much farther. She had to pass through it before the shadow could catch them. Fiona had never seen the shadow move quickly, but she couldn't be sure it wasn't just steps behind them.

The note led to a decaying sassafras tree. A narrow door in its trunk opened. Its branches drooped like the weight of the world was held by its limbs. It needed water and sunlight. No wonder Ferris didn't know about the Great Piano. His portal looked totally cut off from the real world.

Fiona turned sideways to slip through the door. There wasn't time to worry whether she'd fit. She sucked in her stomach.

She wasn't totally sure, but she might've seen a handless arm reach for her just before she was overcome by the dark.

♪♪♪♪♪♪

Fiona didn't stop running, not until she was sure nothing had followed her through the portal. She crouched beside a human-sized mailbox and placed the amphibians on the ground. Even if whatever was following them hadn't made it through the portal, Fugue's key was still in the piano. It could find its way in at any moment. Was the shadow the real reason the piano was missing its keys?

A dull, gray sun hung in the sky. Actually, everything was gray. Fiona, Ferris, and Nori were the only colorful things in the place. Fiona thought about tying her red jacket around her waist to blend in, but there was nothing Ferris or Nori could do to hide their bright colors.

She didn't see any frogs. The world wasn't what she would describe as foggy either, but maybe Fugue had a different definition of the word. "Is this—" Fiona began to ask Ferris if they were in the right place, but when she turned she saw he was being shoved into a cage by a gray man in a police uniform.

"Excuse me! That's my friend, you can't take him away," she protested.

"Don't worry," replied the officer with a smudged grin. "We're taking you with him."

The officer pressed a hand to Fiona's back, forcing her into the back of his car. Nori was already caged inside it. The amphibian shook with fright. Ferris's cage came in next. It was tossed haphazardly as though it held a pair of dirty socks, not a living creature. The officer slammed the door shut.

"What's going on?" Fiona whispered.

Ferris couldn't meet Fiona's gaze. He shook his head. "We're in the wrong place."

The wrong place. How could that be? They'd followed the card reader's instructions to a T, or maybe to a tea if Rina had her way. Fiona sat up straighter. "Sir, where are you taking us? We didn't do anything wrong."

"Quiet!" the police officer snapped. "You know exactly what you did."

But Fiona didn't know. She was just trying to get Ferris home. Out the window of the police car, skyscrapers towered above them. Uniform sedans in three-lane traffic honked as they sped by. The streets were crowded with businesspeople bumping shoulders and briefcases on their way to work. It looked like New York City, except that everything was blurry and two-dimensional. The world they had entered was a messy charcoal drawing. Caricatures, just like Torien said.

The police officer drove furiously through the streets, making everything appear more blurry than before. The only thing Fiona could make out was an imposing trapezoidal building at the center of the city with a giant swinging arm, a metronome. It ticked back and forth so rapidly the arm risked snapping off.

The drive to the police station had been short, but the sun was already setting when they arrived. The officer got out of the driver's seat and opened the back door. He yanked Fiona out by her wrist.

"Can you let go of me? I can walk on my own," Fiona tried.

The officer gripped harder. He grabbed Ferris and Nori's cages with his other hand and dragged the three of them through the lobby of an echoey building and into a vacant elevator.

The officer dropped Ferris and Nori's cages on the floor and kicked them aside as he pressed the button for the one hundred sixteenth floor. Fiona's wrist turned red and black under his charcoal grip. She shifted uncomfortably. Could she get away with a swift karate chop to the officer's hand? Probably not.

The elevator shot up at an impossible speed. Ferris held his stomach like he might be sick. When the elevator stopped moving, its doors opened abruptly to the sound of fingers clacking on keyboards. Obscured faces looked up from their desks, just for a moment, before putting their heads down and returning to work. At the back of the office, were two empty jail cells. The officer threw Fiona and the amphibians into the same cell without letting the Ferris or Nori out of their cages.

He slammed the door shut and said gruffly, "You're hereby sentenced to a year in jail for traveling without a permit."

Nori's mouth dropped open.

"No sir," Ferris began, "Come on. This isn't right. We entered the wrong portal, an honest mistake. We'll go straight back the way we came, just let us out."

"Do you think I haven't heard that before, toad?" The police officer hissed. "Everyone thinks they can sneak into Metronome and draw themselves a pretty little life of whatever they want." The officer twinkled his fingers in the air in a mocking fashion. "That's not how it works. There are rules. There is order. One more word out of you and I'll make it five years in this cell." The officer took a pencil out of the holster on his belt and drew a lock on the cell door. It solidified, becoming three-dimensional right before Fiona's eyes. The officer rattled the door to make sure it was locked securely before turning and striding away with a crooked smile.

Fiona felt like she was coming down with a fever. Her head throbbed. Her teeth clattered. Her face grew hot. She placed clammy hands over her cheeks to cool down. She hadn't done anything wrong. She was sure of it. Yet despite following the rules and doing what she was told, she was in jail for breaking a rule she couldn't have known existed. It didn't make sense.

Outside the cell, office workers moved so quickly it made her dizzy. She sat on the bench against the wall and put her head between her knees. When the feverish feeling passed, she lifted her head and looked to the caged frog. "What's the plan?" she asked, her voice weak and shaky.

Ferris threw his hands up. "There's no plan, Fiona. I trusted you with the key. Look where that got us," he growled. "When we get out of here, leave me to find Fugue alone."

The shock of Ferris's demeanor left Fiona speechless. She put a hand to her stomach to shield herself from the blow. Ferris had never spoken to her that way before. Of course, she was sorry they'd ended up in the wrong place, but she'd put the right key in the piano. She was pretty sure of it anyway. Like ninety percent sure.

She moved her hand to her lower left pocket. The key from the red geyser was still there. She would have put the key to Fugue in the pocket for things she cared about and the mystery key in the pocket for hard-to-lose things. Right? The longer she was in this world, the strangest of all the worlds she had been in so far, the more she began to doubt herself.

Fiona gripped the bench with her hands and swung her feet, trying to piece together where it had all gone wrong, but the puzzle pieces wouldn't fit. Torien said finding the key would be obvious. Fiona and Ferris had agreed that meant finding the key would be easy. It would be obvious to Ferris when he had found the right one. Mari had said the key would be at the yellow geyser. Fiona had followed their instructions and still ended up here. If she couldn't trust adults, who could she count on?

Fiona had entered the woods against her mother's wishes. She couldn't imagine not knowing about the Great Piano now. She'd asked for directions at the bakery. Where would they be without Arti's doorstop key? She'd picked that place for a reason. And she freed Nori, even when Ferris didn't want to. Fiona squared her shoulders. She could trust herself.

It was quiet in the cell. Nori got bored and chased her tail around her cage. The office workers looked to be in some sort of trance. They moved incredibly fast. They typed without pausing to think. They power-walked to the conference room for every meeting. The people were all different shapes, some round and some square, but they all shared crescent moon bags under their eyes.

Every hour, the workers left the office. An hour after that, they returned wearing new clothes. Each time they returned, they raced to the coffee machine for a drink, though if anyone took a sip of the liquid, Fiona didn't see it. Coffee was bitter enough as is. Charcoal coffee had to taste like tar. Just watching the workers was tiring. Fiona laid back on the bench. She threw her jacket over her head to block out the light and fell asleep.

Fiona awoke to the sound of a metal plate being pushed through an opening in the cell door. The plate held a lump of oatmeal. It was handled by a man with a thin but kind smile. Fiona supposed not everyone from Metronome was as mean as the police officer. She picked up the plate and scooped the oatmeal into her mouth. It was exactly as delicious as one might expect charcoal oatmeal to be. It crunched like sand between her teeth. At least she would never have to question what dirt tasted like.

Chapter 16

Ferris and Nori were given a plate of gray worms to share, but for once, Ferris couldn't eat. He cleared his throat. "I'm sorry for before. For yelling. Every time I think I'm home, the lily pad gets pulled out from under me. It's not your fault."

Fiona nodded, taking the apology in. "Thanks. I know it's hard being away from home for so long."

"I imagine you're starting to know that as well as I do. I think you've more than made up for the pickle jar fiasco."

The corner of Fiona's mouth tipped up. It was nice being appreciated.

"I wish I had freckles like you," said a girl from the cell next door.

Heat rose in Fiona's cheeks. She hadn't noticed anyone was in there.

"Green would be cool. Or yellow. Maybe purple," said the girl with a look of glee as she imagined all the colors freckles could be.

This wasn't the first time Fiona had received a compliment about her freckles. It might've even been the third or the fourth time. For a moment, she feared she might get used to the compliments. Could she return to a world where her freckles scared people away? She bulldozed the thought aside.

The girl was about Fiona's age. She had wavy, unbrushed hair and brilliant black eyes. She was more defined than the other people of Metronome. In fact, she was drawn so realistically, she could have almost been part of Fiona's world. The only thing giving her away was some shading on her skin.

"Where are you all from?" the girl asked.

"*Coqui*," said Nori, wagging her tail.

Ferris translated. "Nori is from Chords. I'm from Fugue. Fiona is from Massachusetts."

The girl's eyes twinkled. "I've never been to any of those places. I haven't even heard of Mesa-Chess-Sets. I'm Coda."

FIONA AND THE FORGOTTEN PIANO

Nori extended her hand out from her cage. Coda bent to shake it.

"Why are you here?" asked Ferris bluntly.

The girl's mouth quirked up into a sideways grin. "Oh, I'm here all the time. The mayor is my uncle, and I refuse to follow the pace he sets."

"Do you work for him?" Fiona asked.

"We all do, in a way. As mayor, he gets to choose the speed of the city's metronome. It sets the tempo for everyone. The faster the metronome ticks, the faster we move to keep up with the beat. Our days are only"—she paused to count something out on her fingers—"two hours your time."

Fiona listened for the tick of the metronome. When she heard it, she understood why the workers moved as fast as they did. "But you don't move like everyone else," she said.

Coda's eyes gleamed. She grabbed the bars between their cells and leaned forward. Her voice lowered. "Have you ever been walking down the street, and a car goes by playing loud music and suddenly, you find you're walking to the beat of the music instead of your normal pace?"

Nori shook her head *no*. The axolotl probably hadn't even seen a car until she arrived in Metronome, but Fiona nodded.

"It's hard not to follow the beat, but I found a way to skip some. I only move every third or fourth tick instead of every one."

"Is that why you look more..." Fiona hesitated, not wanting to offend the girl. "Is that why you look more real than the others?"

Coda nodded. "When you're always in a rush, your body can't keep up. Eventually you blur. When people grow old here, they've often spent so much time being blurry they fall apart into a jumble of shapes. It's really sad actually."

Fiona put an uncomfortable hand to her stomach. She couldn't imagine living life that way, like she could fall apart at any moment. And to move so fast she blurred—Fiona's heart nearly stopped. The thing in the fire world, the shadow in the woods, what if it wasn't a shadow but a blur? That would mean—she didn't want to believe it— but that would mean she had entered its world.

"That's awful," said Ferris. He was right but it didn't seem like he'd put together how next-level awful it was. Why would someone from this world be after her?

"It is," Coda agreed. "That's why I'm going to remove my uncle from office and slow the metronome, but it's difficult to do when people can't slow down to think."

Coda kicked at the bars holding her back. They didn't budge. "It's even more difficult to do from jail."

Was slowing the Metronome what Fiona needed to do to get the shadow off her back? That couldn't be what it wanted her for. She had nothing to do with Metronome. It should've followed Coda if that's what it wanted. And if it was something as simple as that, why couldn't it have asked politely? It had to want something else.

As if to change the subject, the elevator doors dinged open. The room grew quiet. The workers stopped talking, keyboards stopped clacking, even the coffee machine stopped bubbling. All that could be heard was the tick-tick-tick of the giant metronome.

An octagonal man in an opaque suit strutted across the office floor. Two bodyguards followed closely behind.

The man stopped an inch from the cell. Fiona stepped up to meet him. He was not much taller than she was. He had thick protruding eyebrows that brushed against the cell bars. His eyes were small and beady. He extended a hand to Fiona. She rubbed the back of her neck, pretending not to see the gesture. Nori stuck her arm out, but if the man noticed, he ignored her. He wrapped his outstretched hand around one of the cell's bars as if that had always been his intention and leaned in closer.

"I can have those erased for you if you like," he said in a low voice, wiggling his finger in the direction of her freckles. Fiona took a step back. "It's a simple procedure. Doubt it would put a hole through your cheeks... though I wouldn't mind finding out," the man said.

"No, thank you." Fiona replied firmly. The insult didn't sting like it normally would. It slid past her like a light breeze.

"I suppose if you're going to spend all your time in jail it won't matter anyway." The man shrugged. "I'm Mayor DaCapo. You may refer to me as such. I hope Mr. Pitman has been kind to you." The mayor gestured to a man pouring coffee beans into the office espresso machine. It was the same man who'd slid the plate of oatmeal into her cell.

Fiona nodded.

"Good. He's usually a halfwit." The mayor chuckled. "Someone must've forgotten to draw the other half of his brain." He continued to laugh at himself. His eyes glared left and right until his bodyguards joined in. Then he shushed them. "Moving on! I know you must be itching to get out of here. However, you broke the rules and—as we say in Metronome—we mustn't draw outside the lines."

Fiona glanced at the mayor's eyebrows and wondered if they qualified as being outside the lines.

The mayor reached to smooth them out and cleared his throat. "Now, I understand you've been here a week and you've got a year on your sentence. I might be able to reduce your time to six months if you're on your best behavior."

"Actually, we've only been here a few hours," Fiona replied in her best grumpy Ferris impersonation.

"No," Mayor DaCapo pursed his lips. "I'm certain you are wrong about that. We keep good records here. What do you think all these people are for?" he said, referring to the office workers who had gotten back to work but were typing much quieter than before.

Liar. The mayor was a liar. He was the one controlling time. He was the reason for the bags under the workers' eyes, the reason Fiona and her friends were in jail, the reason people broke down into nothing. He had the power to fix it but would rather let people suffer. Her hands balled up into fists. Fiona counted the things they had done on her fingers. "We came through the tree portal, got arrested, I took a nap, and now you're here, so really, it has just been a few hours."

"Perhaps you slept longer than you think," Mayor DaCapo said with a smile that didn't touch his eyes or his eyebrows. "Now, the question is, how did you find this place?"

"We didn't mean to come here." Fiona argued. "We were supposed to go to Fugue, and I mixed up the keys." Fiona took the other black key from her pocket. "This is the key to Fugue. We don't need to stay for a year or even six months. Let us out and we'll leave."

Mayor DaCapo examined the key in Fiona's hands. "That's not the key to Fugue," he said.

Fiona furrowed her brow. How did he know?

"I can tell by the vibration it gives off," he said, reaching for the key in Fiona's hand.

She backed away, just a few steps but far enough the mayor couldn't reach her in the cell. "I'm not giving you the key," she said. Finally, her voice sounded as firm as she meant it to.

The mayor guffawed. "You've got to be joking. Hand it over."

"I don't trust you. I just met you, and in the few hours that I've been here, I haven't heard a single good thing about you." Fiona emphasized the word hours. The mayor wasn't going to change her mind about something as irrefutable as time. She set her jaw. Strength rushed through her like a tidal wave. She hadn't stuck up to anyone like this before, let alone an adult. It felt surprisingly like relief.

There was a sharp intake of breath. It had come from Ferris. Fiona's eyes flicked towards his cage. It was shocking, she knew, for her to stand up to someone like this. She hoped Ferris approved of what she'd said. She couldn't take it back even if she wanted to. And she didn't want to.

The girl in the cell next door didn't know this was unusual behavior for Fiona. A pleased smirk crawled up Coda's face, like she couldn't wait to see how her uncle would react.

The mayor's lips turned up into a sly grin. He spoke slowly. "Give me the key or I'll have you locked away in the dark cell."

Fiona didn't know what that meant, but she could tell it was something the mayor was used to saying to get his way. She wasn't from here though. She wasn't afraid of him. She crossed her arms and said simply, "No."

The weight of the word hung in the air.

"You only say no," DaCapo's voice began to shake with anger, "because you don't know what the dark cell is."

Fiona stood her ground. She didn't know what the dark cell was. But she could guess it was a cell that was dark.

"The dark cell is impenetrable to light or sound. Many have lost their minds in it. Some become one with the darkness and never come out, even if we let them." DaCapo extended his hand for the key once again.

Fiona wasn't going to budge. She'd blindly done what people expected of her for too long. She glared at the mayor.

"Open the gate!" DaCapo shouted at his bodyguards.

The bodyguards fumbled for the keyrings in their pockets in a race to do DaCapo's bidding. The larger of the two came out victorious and opened the cell door. DaCapo stepped through it.

Fiona clutched the key in her hand so tightly her nails dug into her palm and her knuckles turned white.

"You've got one more chance to hand over the key," said the mayor, inching closer to Fiona as if he might grab her at any second.

She stuffed her closed fist into her pocket for another layer of protection. "You can take me to the dark cell, but you're not getting this key."

Mayor DaCapo let out an awkward giggle. He looked at Ferris's and Nori's cages on the ground. "You know what?" He tapped Nori's cage with his foot. "I've had a change of heart. Keep your key, but I'm taking this rat as collateral."

The mayor's octagonal body folded forward as he lifted Nori's cage. She squealed in fright. The amphibian backed as far into the cage as she could, but it didn't help. DaCapo grinned at her with a wide, contemptuous grin, his eyebrows poking through the cage bars. "You're going to hate the dark cell."

"Wait!" Fiona yelled. Nori couldn't get stuck in another prison. She'd already been caged in ice and now charcoal. How would she fare in a cell that drove people mad? Fiona grabbed at DaCapo's hands, trying to pull Nori back from him, but the cage and the mayor's hand had become one.

"Fine, take the key!" Fiona said, pulling it from her pocket.

"Grab it," DaCapo ordered his guards.

They took the key from Fiona and passed it to DaCapo.

"You have to give Nori back now," said Fiona.

"I don't, actually." DaCapo said and he crushed the key in his hand. It turned to charcoal dust as it fell to the floor.

"No!" Fiona clambered after DaCapo, but the bodyguards grabbed her arms and pushed her back onto the cell bench. She tried to wriggle out of their grip. She kicked and screamed, but their powerful arms were drawn with unyielding muscles. She didn't have a chance. The bodyguards held Fiona down until DaCapo got in the elevator with Nori. He gave an infuriating little wave as the doors closed.

Chapter 17

The jail cell on the one hundred and sixteenth floor bubbled over with feelings like a shaken-up soda bottle. Fiona herself was a bubble, not sure whether she'd release a scream or a puddle of tears when her delicate exterior burst. She was losing hope she could help Ferris. She'd sent Nori to the dark cell. If only she had kept her mouth shut.

"How could you know what my uncle was going to do? You couldn't know he was going to take Nori," said Coda, trying to reassure her.

"That doesn't make it right," said Fiona weakly. "I was trying to stand up for myself for once, and I brought Nori down with me. She didn't deserve that."

Ferris cleared his throat. "Does us no good sitting around being sad about it. We need a plan. I need a way out of this cage. Then we can save Nori."

Fiona closed her eyes and rubbed her hands over her temples in thought. Ferris was right. She could cry about Nori, or she could save her friend. She turned to Coda. "How do we get Ferris out?"

"You need an eraser," answered Coda.

"How do we get that?"

"You've got two options. We can steal one, or you can use your superpower."

"Our what?" asked Ferris unamused.

Coda turned sideways and became as thin as a piece of paper. She stepped through the bars of the cell to join Fiona.

Fiona stuck her neck out in surprise. She now understood why Coda was so nonchalant about being in jail. Coda wasn't trapped the same way she and Ferris were. Still, there were probably other consequences of escaping Fiona didn't know about. Maybe leaving this jail sent someone straight to the dark cell.

"Why do you think DaCapo is so afraid of outsiders?" Coda said. "Our world is made of charcoal. Outsiders have something we don't."

Fiona stared blankly at Coda.

Coda put a hand on Fiona's shoulder. "You have spit."

Spit.

Spit in a charcoal world.

Fiona broke into a smile. Was it that simple? Could a bit of water could erase the things that stood in their way? If she and Ferris had erasers on their side, they'd be practically unstoppable. Not to mention it would be a good defense if they were to come up against the shadow. This was the hope she needed.

Fiona looked to Ferris to see if he understood too. He was already wiping at one of his cage's bars with a sticky frog foot.

"Even with your superpower, we'll need a careful plan to escape," Coda continued. "Metronomians can draw faster than you can erase. If you're caught, they'll put you in the dark cell too," she shivered.

"Where is the dark cell?" Fiona asked.

Coda's eyes darted from one end of the room to the other. The workers had gone home again so no one was around, but still, she lowered her voice. "I've heard rumors that DaCapo keeps a close eye on his captives. He likes to... watch them lose their minds." She swallowed, probably ashamed she was related to the man. "I think the dark cell is in his office. It's only a few blocks from here."

Fiona nodded solemnly. "If we go to DaCapo's office, we can save Nori and slow the metronome." And there was the part she didn't say out loud. Fiona hoped that in doing all this, she could figure out what the shadow wanted too. She certainly couldn't wait for it to find her in jail.

Fiona, Ferris, and Coda hatched a plan. The next time the workers went home, they would free themselves and find a place to hide until the following night. Of course, the next night would only be an hour later since apparently even the sun followed the metronome's tempo. They would then break into DaCapo's office, slow the metronome, free Nori, stop the shadow, and find the key to Fugue. If it sounded like an impossible plan, it's probably because it was. Fiona was crazy to believe they could do all that in the span of a few hours. But letting the rules dictate what she should do wasn't an option anymore. There was too much at stake not to try something. To make matters even more impossible, they would need to find a pencil so they could disguise themselves. The police would be looking for them after all.

"Doesn't everyone have a pencil?" Ferris asked Coda.

"Not here. Pencils are only given to people with certain authority, like police officers and security guards. They're the only ones DaCapo trusts."

♪♪♪♪♪♪

The arms on the wall clock zipped around its face. Fiona waited for the moment it would hit 5 p.m. when the workers would leave. At home, time passed slowly when she was waiting for something. That wasn't the case in Metronome. What if they didn't have enough time to carry out their plan? It was a silly thing to worry about. Of course, they didn't have enough time. That was the entire reason DaCapo ran the city the way he did, so no one would have enough time for anything.

When the clock hit four, the workers checked their emails one last time. They dumped their full coffee cups down the sink and turned off their computers. Fiona licked her fingertips. In another minute, the clock turned five and the workers rushed out of the building, piling in the elevators like sardines.

The moment the elevator doors closed, Fiona rubbed her wet fingers over Ferris's cage, clearing away the smudges he'd left with his feet. What was left of the bars slid apart. He was free.

Ferris hopped out of his cage and sprang into action. He leapt to the top of the cell. It was the highest Fiona had ever seen him jump. He grabbed hold of one of the bars and slid down it like a firefighter. If Ferris believed in their half-baked plan, she would too.

The mucus on the frog's feet faded the charcoal, but it wasn't enough. The bars were still solid. He jumped again.

Fiona worked on a second bar. They only needed to erase a few before she'd be able to squeeze out of the cell. Her fingertips alone were not enough this time. She licked her palms and dragged them over the bars like a reverse paintbrush.

Coda paced around the cell talking to herself, or at least Fiona hoped it was to herself because she was too focused to listen. "I don't think we can steal a pencil from a police officer. They're too skilled anyway. They'd draw up another jail in seconds. I bet DaCapo doesn't guard his pencils—no one would dare steal from him—but we'll need to get a hold of one before we get to his office." The charcoal girl sat on the floor in a huff. She put her head in her hands. "The kitchen! They need pencils to make food. They're probably downstairs making breakfast right now."

Under the thin layer of black accumulating on Fiona's hands, her skin turned a light shade of pink. No one ever said having a superpower was easy. The cell's bars put up a fight against the spit. The charcoal's gritty texture felt like sandpaper. With each lick of her palms, the flavor of earth and smoke filled her mouth. She didn't stop working to reply. Her words were muffled between licks. "Was the chef the man who gave me oatmeal this morning? Mr. Pitman?"

"Exactly! The kitchen is on the fourth floor. We can stop there on our way out."

Fiona was nervous about stealing, especially from one of the few people that had been nice to her in Metronome. But what other options did they have? She couldn't leave Nori in the dark cell; she couldn't keep Ferris away from Fugue; and she couldn't be captured by a creepy shadow blur person thing.

Coda must've noticed worry lines in Fiona's face because she said, "Look, we're going to be doing the guy a favor. We need the pencil to slow the metronome, and he'll be happier when we do that."

"Couldn't we just ask him to borrow it?" Fiona asked.

"We don't have time for that. Mr. Pitman doesn't break rules. We'd spend so much time trying to convince him we need the pencil that the police would find us."

Fiona's stomach gurgled. She thought it was due to her unease over Coda's plan, but it might've been that she'd accidentally eaten more charcoal. "Okay, but you'll give the pencil back to him when we're done?"

"Definitely! I'll take one of DaCapo's pencils once we break into his office anyway, so I won't need a second one."

Fiona found herself rolling her eyes, she was starting to see why Coda ended up in jail so often. At least the girl had good intentions.

Just then, Fiona's hands broke through the cell bars. She stumbled forward into the office. Fiona wasn't normally claustrophobic, but she knew what it was like to feel held back. When the bars were scrubbed away, she felt like she was shaking off years of strict barriers and unreasonable rules. She took a relieving breath. It caught in her throat, and she coughed up the charcoal taste in her lungs.

"You did it!" Coda exclaimed, hugging Fiona.

Fiona tried to hug Coda back, but there wasn't much to hug. Coda's two-dimensional body made it feel as though Fiona was being gift wrapped in old newspaper. It was awkward, but still, it felt nice to make a new friend.

Ferris bolted for the elevator. He left tiny charcoal footprints across the office floor. Any workers arriving early for their shift would know immediately that they'd broken free. But there was no time to conceal the evidence of their escape. Inside the elevator, Coda pressed the glowing button for the fourth floor. Ferris held his stomach in anticipation of the drop, and the elevator cascaded downwards.

Chapter 18

The elevator doors opened to an empty cafeteria. Two rows of tables neatly lined the room. The tables closest to Fiona had clean lines and crisp edges, but the ones farther away appeared fuzzy.

"The kitchen is this way," said Coda pointing to a swinging door behind empty buffet tables.

As the trio moved to the back of the room, Fiona's perspective changed as if she were entering a new drawing with each step she took. The tables nearest to her were always the most distinct and lifelike. But the ones by the elevator no longer looked real at all. From this angle, Fiona doubted they would even hold up under Ferris's weight.

A small, square window in the kitchen door revealed shadows moving beyond it. Any one of them could be the shadow following Fiona. Or maybe that one would emerge silently from the elevator. Fiona shook her head of the thought. She needed to focus. Nori was in trouble. She'd evaded the shadow for this long, she could keep avoiding it until she saved her friend.

Muffled shouts snuck out from behind the kitchen door. She and Coda crouched beside it. Being small, Ferris didn't need to crouch, but he did anyway—the situation called for it. Very slowly and very quietly, Coda pushed the door open. Just a crack, just enough to see through it.

The voice of Mr. Pitman projected through the opening. "We need two thousand eggs, one thousand strips of bacon, and three thousand oranges. Bell and Reed, start drawing them up. Pipa and I will get cooking as soon as you've got a few dozen each."

"Heard!" the chefs replied in unison.

"And don't get lazy with your ovals," Mr. Pitman continued. "I need eggs, not ping pong balls."

"Yes, chef," replied two voices presumably belonging to Bell and Reed.

Coda released her hold on the door. "There's four of them. Two are doing prep work. They're the ones with pencils. Mr. Pitman and the other chef can't start working until they've drawn enough food, so if we want a pencil now, we need a distraction."

Fiona scratched her head. She still had charcoal on her hands. Undoubtedly, she now had a giant black streak across her forehead as well. "I have an idea," she said. "Can you see the light switch in there?"

Coda wrapped her fingers around the underside of the door and pulled it open again. Mr. Pitman arranged pans on the stove. Two prep cooks drew eggs in the air and caught them before they fell to the table. A fourth chef pieced together a machine with more parts than seemed necessary. "The light switch is next to the fridge on the right," Coda said.

"Got it," Fiona said and then swallowed. If she thought too much about what she was going to do, she might chicken out. It seemed better to blurt out her idea so she couldn't take it back. Fiona had put Nori in the dark cell, it was her responsibility to get the axolotl out of it, even if it meant stealing or going back to jail. "I'll sneak in and turn off the lights. Then I'll cover the light switch and make it disappear." She held up her blackened hands. "They won't be able to turn the lights back on, so they'll have to stop working. And Ferris is really good at seeing in the dark, so he'll get the pencil. We'll escape before they even know we're here."

Ferris, surprisingly, had no arguments. He simply nodded. Fiona gave a pinched smile. She wouldn't let the frog down this time.

"Great. What about me?" Coda asked, excitement plain on her face. For a moment, Fiona was tempted to let Coda be the one to turn out the lights. By the looks of it, she would do it in a heartbeat. But Fiona had the blackened hands, and she couldn't let others do her dirty work.

"You can be the lookout," Fiona said, hoping the role would appease Coda.

"It's the middle of the night, who do I need to look out for?" she objected.

Fiona faltered. "I... don't know, but that's the point isn't it? We won't know if someone's coming, so you have to look out for us."

"Fine." Coda said flatly. "But give me your coat, you're not sneaking anywhere with that thing."

Fiona removed her brightly colored coat and handed it to Coda. But her jacket wasn't the only thing bright about her. She put an anxious hand to her cheek. If only she could hand her freckles to Coda too. She imagined plucking them off like stickers and sprinkling them in Coda's open palm.

Coda rolled her eyes reassuringly. "If they're looking at your face, you've already been caught."

Fiona blushed. That was true. And she wouldn't be caught. She couldn't. She took Coda's place by the door and peered through it. One cook drew strips of bacon as long as the table. The other divided the strips into smaller pieces. Mr. Pitman was preparing to crack the eggs. Fiona had to get to the light switch before any food hit the stove. She couldn't risk starting a fire.

She crawled through the door, holding her fists closed to ensure the charcoal stayed on her palms. The drawn tile floor was surprisingly cold and hard against her elbows. What would happen if she began to sweat? Would it erase the tiles? Would she fall through the floor? She paused behind a trash can and dabbed her forehead with the back of her forearm. No sweat yet.

Fiona made herself small. She hugged her knees and kept her head low. She eyed the growing pile of eggshells on Mr. Pitman's station. She had to move before he tossed them in the trash and found her curled up beside it like a hungry rat. She waited for an opening when the chefs were distracted. Finally, Bell and Reed joined Mr. Pitman at the stove to cook the strips of bacon they'd drawn. Fiona inched toward the refrigerator.

The fourth chef, whom Fiona had determined was named Pipa, gathered plates from the dishwashing station. She stacked them forty high, blocking her view of the floor in front of her. Fiona made her way across the kitchen floor in a zigzag pattern, narrowly avoiding Pipa's wavering footsteps. She slipped into the space between the refrigerator and a table stacked with flatware and condiments. All four chefs were on the other side of the appliance. Fiona reached a blackened hand to the light switch and flipped it off just as Pipa put the plates on the table. The room went dark.

"Argh! What happened now?" shouted one of the chefs.

"Pipa probably bumped the switch. She's always carrying more than she can handle," said another.

"I did not!" Pipa shouted back.

"Turn it back on anyway," replied Mr. Pitman.

Fiona rubbed her hands over the wall where she hoped the light switch was. The sound of footsteps drew nearer. Fiona laid against the wall holding her breath. She could just make out a stealthy amphibious silhouette sneaking its way to the prep table.

Fiona heard Pipa slapping the wall above her in various spots, growing more and more frantic. She couldn't find the light switch. The plan was working.

"Something happened," Pipa said. "The switch is gone."

"Pipa, seriously? We don't have time for games," a chef complained.

"I'm not kidding, come take a look if you don't believe me," she replied. *Please don't*, thought Fiona. She couldn't hold her breath much longer. She didn't need the whole kitchen investigating her work.

"Alright," Mr. Pitman said, putting an end to the bickering. "The electricity must've gone out. I'm turning off the stove. The generator will kick on in a minute. Let's clear out."

Oh no.

That wasn't good either. Fiona hadn't considered the chefs might leave the kitchen. Coda was right outside the door. She racked her brain for a way out of the situation. She wished she'd planned for this. Should she knock something over? Falling pots would make a loud, startling clang. Maybe they wouldn't notice Coda then.

But it was too late. The door swung open, and the chefs exited the kitchen.

"Coda!" Mr. Pitman jumped, putting a hand to his chest. "What are you doing here?"

"Oh! I was"—Coda fumbled to think of an excuse. She stood up quickly and hid Fiona's jacket behind her back—"hoping to get some breakfast. The early bird gets the crispiest bacon, right?"

"I thought you had a week left on your sentence," Mr. Pitman said through squinted eyes.

"Nope—got off on good behavior. I can see you're having electricity problems though, so I'll just stop by later." Coda backed away towards the elevator. Then she paused. Her friends would need time to escape. She stopped backing up and asked, "Do you want to hear a very long story?"

"No, thank you," replied Mr. Pitman, cracking open a can of soda he'd pulled from the pocket of his apron.

"Right, that makes sense. How about a short, but very loud story?" Coda tried.

"Also no," said Reed.

"Fair enough. How about we all block our ears and hum our favorite song. See if you can guess what everyone else is humming with your ears covered."

Coda was very obviously running out of ideas. But maybe the chefs would want to play the game because it actually did sound fun.

"It would be really helpful if you could notify facilities that our electricity is out," Pipa said. She raised her eyebrows expectantly.

Coda's eyes flitted to the kitchen door. She'd overestimated how easily these chefs could be distracted. Hopefully, Fiona and Ferris had figured something out. "Yep. Totally. Facilities, Fifty-second floor. I'll go there now," she replied.

She turned slowly and walked to the elevator, moving casually enough not to raise suspicions, though it was possible Mr. Pitman caught a flash of red as she left.

Chapter 19

Ferris had located the pencils in the kitchen. "Should we take them both?" he whispered.

Fiona shook her head. She wanted to explain that they shouldn't take away the chefs' ability to do their jobs. She didn't know what kind of punishment that would lead to. She and Ferris would be slower with one pencil, but at least the chefs could finish making breakfast. Except Fiona couldn't say all that because the chefs were right outside the door, and she couldn't risk making that much noise.

They needed a way out of the kitchen. On the other side of the door, Coda was making conversation with the chefs. Hopefully she had some clever way to distract them. Fiona figured it was safe enough to whisper. "Can you draw a door?" she asked Ferris.

"This pencil is twice the size of me. You should do it," Ferris whispered back. He slid the pencil into Fiona's hand.

She drew a wide doorway and a dividing line down the center of it. Next to the doors, she drew a button with an arrow. Within seconds, the lines of Fiona's drawing transformed from faint scratches into something lifelike. She pressed the newly drawn button and was pleasantly surprised when it compressed.

The doors slid open. A beam of light brightened the kitchen. A bell chimed. Fiona winced, hoping the chefs hadn't heard it. It was an elevator just like the one they'd used to arrive on this floor. The inside was complete with handrails and buttons to each floor of the building, even though Fiona hadn't drawn them. It was like the world had filled in the missing pieces. At least she hoped that's how it worked because she hadn't drawn any of the motors or pulleys that make elevators actually function. She didn't share this thought with Ferris as they stepped into the elevator. The doors closed behind them.

"Now what?" asked the frog.

"Stick with the plan. We have to find a place to hide for the day. We'll find Nori at night," Fiona said.

"What about Coda?" Ferris asked.

"She'll be okay. She knows this place better than any of us." Fiona looked at the elevator panel and debated which button to push. It had floors one through two hundred. That had to be more floors than the Empire State Building. With two hundred floors full of people, Fiona and Ferris were bound to be caught if they stayed put. Their best option was to hide in a different building entirely.

On the panel, there was an L for lobby. They couldn't go there; the lobby had security guards who would take them back to jail. There was a B for basement, but basements don't always have an easy way out. Fiona pressed the M for mezzanine. Mezzanines were like balconies. They might be able to see into the lobby without the guards seeing them from that floor.

The elevator descended with a whoosh. Ferris flattened himself against the floor. He spread his limbs out wide. He appeared to be praying that the contents of his stomach would stay put.

With a ping, the doors opened. Fiona peeked out. She didn't see any guards. She exited the elevator, still surprised it had worked. Ferris followed. They stood in a darkened hallway with bumpy textured walls. Unmarked doors lined the hall on either side of them. Fiona swallowed. It was the perfect place for the shadow to find her.

"Ferris, do you think...?" She was afraid to speak the words out loud. What if the shadow heard her?

"Yes," Ferris said too quickly. It might've been sarcasm. He was probably about to say that of course frogs think. Instead he said, "I think the shadow is from here."

Fiona bit her cheek. She thought it would feel good to share her suspicions, but it only made her more nervous that Ferris agreed. "So... get out of here as fast as possible?"

"Was always my intention," Ferris said.

It was Fiona's intention too. As soon as she'd seen the distinct lack of frogs in headlamps, she'd wanted to leave. This place with its made-up rules and its ridiculous schedules had kept her and Ferris away from home for far too long. And now they couldn't leave without Nori. She'd saved them from Chords. It was their turn to save her from Metronome. "Maybe there's an exit through here," Fiona said in a hushed tone as she shuffled down the row of doors.

"Why don't you draw a door out of here?" Ferris asked.

Fiona's mouth pulled to one side. "I'm not sure it works that way. When I drew the elevator doors, I didn't know where they would take us or what buttons would be inside. It's like the world made sense of them. The elevator became part of the building. If I drew a door here"—Fiona

FIONA AND THE FORGOTTEN PIANO

gestured to the air in front of her—"I think when we opened it, it would just lead to the hallway behind it."

Ferris cocked his head. "How about a window then?"

Fiona considered it. "It's worth a shot." Windows were easy to draw anyway.

Against the wall and not too high off the ground, Fiona drew a square with a cross through it. The wall behind it faded away into nothing. Dull sunlight filtered in. It peered through the newly drawn window and illuminated a sliver of hallway. The sun was rising. It was too late to find another place to hide. This dark hallway, whatever it was, would have to suffice as their hideout until the sun went down again.

"She's drawn us a window," whispered a small, child-like voice.

"I don't think they belong here," whispered another in a husky tone. "There's nothing wrong with them."

"How did they get so un-gray?" the child-like voice asked.

"Did they invent colored pencils?" asked the husky one.

Fiona and Ferris glanced at each other anxiously. In the empty hallway, the two voices were not as quiet as they thought they were. But the voices couldn't be coming from security guards, or Fiona and Ferris would be in handcuffs already. And the shadow had never been one for using its big person words. "Hello?" she ventured.

A door at the end of the hallway creaked open. A pair of furry pointed ears poked out of it, followed by a set of large eyes and a wet nose. It was a dog, maybe.

"It's okay," said Fiona. "You can come out. We're not going to hurt you."

The creature padded toward Fiona with its head down and eyed her cautiously. It sniffed her feet. Then it turned its nose to Ferris. He held his hand up.

"Excuse me. I don't care to be sniffed," Ferris said.

"Sorry," said the maybe dog. "I'm trying to figure out what's wrong with you."

"Wrong with us?" asked an offended Ferris.

"Well, you're here," said the maybe dog, his head bowed. "You're not a police officer checking in on us or a chef with leftovers, so you must be a mess up."

"A what?" Ferris said in a louder-than-usual tone. Fiona put him on her shoulder, so he'd calm down.

"A mess up." The maybe dog tilted his head. "You know, when someone draws something and it's not right, they have to start over."

Fiona had been wrong about the M in the elevator. It didn't lead to a mezzanine. Maybe it stood for motel. She saw now that each door along the hall had a room number on it. And she didn't like to judge, but if it were a motel, it would be quite a dingy one. "How many of you are there?"

"Fewer than there used to be," the maybe dog said. He scratched his ear with his back leg. Bits of charcoal flaked off him. "It used to be that everyone had pencils until the mayor took them away. He moved us up here, called us mess ups and hasn't let us out since. Welcome to Mess Hall. We don't belong in Metronome, but we have nowhere else to go."

Despite the maybe dog's cheery tone, Fiona's heart tore a little at the edges. She'd only just met him, but she wanted to pat his little head. It sounded like he'd been living in this poorly lit hallway eating scraps from the kitchen for a long time. "I don't mean to pry, but are you a dog?" she asked.

The maybe dog cocked his head. "Not sure. My creator wanted a pet, but she didn't know what kind she wanted. I could be a dog or a cat, a fox maybe. That's why I'm a mess up. DaCapo says no one can tell if I'm a house pet or if I belong in a zoo. I'm just Yip."

The mayor sounded worse with each story Fiona heard about him. If he were a villain in a superhero comic, he'd be called something like Mr. Octagon or Mayor Darkness. Fiona shuddered. "We're looking for a place to stay, just for the day. Do you think we could hide out here?"

"Of course!" Yip said. "Let me introduce you to my friends." He hopped down the hallway and knocked on a few doors. "Come out, we have visitors!"

No doors opened.

"Sorry," Yip shrugged. "They're a little self-conscious. We're not used to being around such well-drawn folks."

"Oh, we're not drawn," said Fiona. "I'm from"—she wasn't going to say Massachusetts again—"outside the woods, and Ferris is from Fugue."

"How'd you end up here?" asked Yip.

Fiona sighed. "We were trying to get Ferris back home. I mixed up the keys, and now DaCapo is keeping our friend in the dark cell."

"It's not Fiona's fault," Ferris admitted. "I thought the note sounded wrong, but there wasn't time to swap out the key. Something from your world was chasing us. Fiona saved us from it."

"Something from our world?" Yip asked.

"A shadow, or a blur of some kind," Fiona clarified.

Yip's ears dipped forward. "You sure? Charcoal and water don't mix well, you know. There's whole bedtime stories about what happens if drawings leave Metronome."

Fiona twisted her fingers around themselves. The shadow had to be from Metronome. It had so much in common with the people here. It had no color. It left a blur behind as it moved. But if Yip says drawings can't leave Metronome... Was it another scare tactic? A rumor spread by the mayor? Or was it possible the shadow was from yet another world? Eighty-eight worlds is a lot, but each one she'd seen had been unique. It didn't seem likely the shadow could be so similar to the Metronomians and be from another place entirely. "Have you ever tried to leave?" she asked.

Yip shook his head vigorously. "I don't want to become a mud puddle!"

Fiona was reminded of her catapult from Torien's roller skates. She glanced at her pants to see if any mud remained. It did. "I was a mud puddle once," she laughed, stretching her pants to show Yip the stain. "It wasn't so bad."

"She fell through a tunnel in the ocean too," Ferris teased.

"So you are a mess up?" Yip chuckled.

Fiona shrugged. "I guess you could say that."

It was exactly what the other mess ups needed to hear. The dormitory doors opened in greeting. Out of one door, a balding unicorn of unexpected proportion trotted forward. "I'm Laika," he said, shaking his mane. His voice was the husky one Fiona had heard earlier. "It's short for 'like a unicorn.' My creator drew my horn first. Then he realized he didn't know how to draw a horse, so my body is too big for my legs, and he never finished my hair."

"Who said a unicorn had to be a horse?" asked Fiona encouragingly. "Have you heard of rhinoceroses? They are big and strong. They have one horn just like you."

Laika whinnied.

A mermaid rolled forward, greeting Fiona in her kiddie pool on wheels. Understandably, it was impossible for her creator to draw the entire ocean. Though a mobile pool seemed like a fun invention. Fiona was surprised she hadn't seen one in Electronica.

From down the hall, the top half of a chicken squawked something that sounded like hello. "Her creator drew the egg she hatched from instead of legs," the mermaid explained.

That seemed like it could've been fixed easily enough. If DaCapo wanted to, he could find it within himself to draw chicken legs. But that would be too kind a gesture for Mayor Darkness.

Yip showed Fiona their rooms, which acted as storage units for unwanted things. The maybe dog's room held a television without wires, a swing set with misshapen seats, and a birthday cake with candles that couldn't be blown out. Despite his living conditions, Yip was optimistic. "I just pretend I'm watching TV," he explained. "And I can

FIONA AND THE FORGOTTEN PIANO

use the swings if I wrap my legs around the seat." He demonstrated how he sat on the swing. It didn't look the least bit comfortable. "And even though frosting is my favorite food, and I can't eat this cake, the candles give me some light."

"I could help you eat it," Fiona said, licking her finger and wiping out the candles. The room dimmed. Fiona frowned. "Sorry. I'll draw a light to make up for that."

"Frosting!" Yip bounced, not caring about the lost candlelight.

"You don't know how long I've been craving cake," said Laika from the doorway.

Yip sniffed the cake excitedly. "Don't worry. I'll share it."

The mermaid entered the room apologetically. "I have this knife. It's dull but you don't need a sharp one to cut cake."

The chicken flew in clasping a crooked plate in her beak. She fluttered back and forth to her room a few more times. Each time she returned with a plate more uneven than the last. She jutted her neck out to hand them off. Fiona supposed she could hold her plate sideways to eat off it.

Laika dragged in a handful of chickpea chairs. "They're like bean bag chairs, but they're better for eating hummus in," the unicorn said through gritted teeth as he pulled a chair across the floor.

As the mess ups ate their cake, Fiona told them about the journey she and Ferris had been on. When she got to the part about Coda, Yip's ears perked up.

"What does she look like?" he asked.

"Long... hair," Fiona had to think about her answer. Everyone here was the color of charcoal and canvas. Describing Coda's eye color or hair color or skin color wouldn't be helpful. "She's bold—but not bold like thick lines. Bold like brave. She buzzes with energy even though she moves slower than everyone else, and she doesn't care what people think about her."

"That's her, my creator!" Yip cried. "Can I come with you to the mayor's office? Please, please, please! I haven't seen her in so long. I bet I can even help you find her."

Fiona glanced at the sun setting outside. "You can join us, but we should get going soon. I'll draw us a ladder so we can climb out the window when it's dark."

Laika whispered something to Yip.

"One more thing before we go—it's a favor." Yip lifted a paw. "Can you draw us some things to make this place feel like home?"

Fiona's heart surged. Finally, there was something she could help with. Since arriving in Metronome, she'd felt like she'd been one tick away from disaster. Now, she could at least leave the mess ups better off than she'd found them. She shook her hair out of her face.

In the mess ups' rooms, she drew big windows with luxurious curtains. She drew chandeliers and art and fluffy carpets in the hallway. They were fancier than the things she had at home, but she hoped the mess ups would appreciate them. They certainly deserved them after what they'd been through. And if the drawings were going to be stuck in this hall a while longer, they'd need things to do too. Fiona drew Laika an apple tree, something he could take care of and eat from. She drew the mermaid a jacuzzi and a pet goldfish. She drew the chicken a giant loaf of bread and a jetpack for when her wings grew tired. The chicken clucked in a way Fiona hoped meant "jetpacks are cooler than legs."

Fiona wasn't quite sure when she'd gotten good at drawing, but all of her creations seemed to work. Who knew building hot tubs and jetpacks was so easy?

When it was time to leave, Fiona drew herself a trench coat—this one with six pockets and a hood. She missed her red jacket, but Coda would keep it safe. Or she might steal it for herself, but she probably wouldn't lose it. Fiona put Ferris in the trench coat's upper left pocket as Yip pushed open the window with his front paws. She drew a long ladder which she slid through the open window into the charcoal night. With her head out the window, she paused to admire the sky. It was like the moon had scribbled over the canvas.

"Miss Fiona, do you think I could hop in one of your pockets too? I can't climb ladders."

Fiona grinned. Yip didn't understand that maybe dogs don't fit in pockets. But she didn't hold it against him. It wasn't like he got out much.

Chapter 20

A few straggling commuters raced home from work. Fiona knew most of them were too busy to notice the colorful, out of place trio, but she told Ferris to keep his head down anyway. She pulled her hood over her hair and held the pencil to her cheek. It would be so easy to wipe her freckles away, so easy to blend in with everyone else.

But she couldn't bring herself to do it. Looking at the people rushing by around her, she didn't want to be just another brushstroke in the crowd. She didn't want to become a rule-following, keyboard-clacking coffee drinker. She certainly didn't want to do that every day until she became only the broken-down shapes of a person. She wanted to be herself, or this new version of herself she'd become since discovering the Great Piano. A world-traveling, volcano-dodging, pencil-wielding friend. Her freckles were a part of that. She tucked the pencil in her pocket.

Then she looked at Yip. "Will people recognize you as a mess up?"

"Only if they get close. I'll stay behind you if they do," he said, wagging his tail. Of course the maybe dog was excited. He was free. He was about to be reunited with his creator. Fiona on the other hand was still unsure if they'd be able to free Nori and avoid the shadow. And if they broke into the mayor's office, it would be selfish of her not to at least try to slow the Metronome. Things were piling up in her head. But these weren't questions. She couldn't just let them out. She had to forge ahead.

From inside the trench coat came Ferris's muffled voice. "Can you sniff out the mayor's office?" he asked.

"Oh," Yip's tail sagged. "I was kind of hoping to find Coda first."

"Coda knew we were headed there," Fiona reassured him. "I'm sure she's thought of a way to meet up with us."

"Okay. Well, his office shouldn't be too hard to find. I know it's in the Metronome building."

"Let's go then." Ferris wriggled around the bottom of Fiona's pocket as if he could propel her forward with the movement.

Yip tilted his head up and sniffed the air. A light breeze ruffled his fur, but it didn't seem to distract him. "The mayor smells like oak, cigars, and bad memories," Yip said. "I could find that scent in a storm. I just need to—" The maybe dog wrinkled his nose. "There it is." Yip bounded after the familiar smell. Fiona imagined it was traveling on a piece of dust carried by the wind.

She ran after Yip with one hand on her head, keeping her hood in place and her brown hair hidden. The fabric in the upper left coat pocket wrinkled from Ferris's grip as he struggled to remain in place.

Maybe in most towns, people stop to help when they see a girl running after her dog, but in Metronome, everyone ran. They probably ran to the gym so they could run on a treadmill. Fiona didn't stand out in the slightest.

The dust led Yip. Yip led Fiona. And Fiona carried Ferris to the giant metronome at the center of the city. When they arrived, the streets had mostly cleared. Overworked Metronomians were likely settling down for an evening that would pass too quickly.

All except for Coda.

And the security guard chasing her.

Coda and the hexagonal security guard blew by Fiona so quickly there was nothing she could do to help. Coda wasn't her usual self. She was blurry like the other

Metronomians. Instead of her free-spirited hair, there was just a rectangle on a round head. Instead of expressive black eyes, there were two dots. If Fiona's red jacket hadn't been tied around the girl's shoulders, she wouldn't have even known it was her. The image sent shivers down her spine.

Yip took off after her. Three blurry figures circled the building. Fiona went dizzy trying to focus on them. She wrapped her arms around herself.

"What's going on?" asked Ferris, hearing the commotion from his place inside the trench coat pocket.

Fiona pulled him out of it. "Coda's in trouble, and Yip took off."

"Get the pencil," Ferris said. "Next time they come around, draw a line between Coda and the guard to trip him."

Fiona bit her lip. Getting the timing of that right would be difficult. But she had to act fast. It wasn't clear how much longer Coda could run like that. The guard had almost certainly called for backup. Fiona's hands trembled a little as she took the pencil from her lower left pocket. In another second, Coda ran by. Fiona drew a line straight through the air. She had meant to draw a tripwire, but in her haste, she drew the line too vertical. It became a wall.

Though the wall worked just as well. The officer ran straight into it. He bumped his head and fell to the ground. Ferris inspected the officer. He had a dent in the canvas of his forehead where he'd hit the accidental wall and was out cold.

Coda slowed and turned around. After a few ticks of the metronome, she morphed into her old, detailed self. Fiona's heart settled with relief. "Haha, good one!" Coda cheered when she saw the wall Fiona created.

But Fiona didn't feel good about it. Her brows furrowed, "What do we do?" she asked, unable to take her eyes off the concussed officer.

Coda came to Fiona's side. Seeing the officer, she put her hands on her hips. "Let's tie him up and hide him behind the bushes," she replied a little too gleefully for Fiona. An involuntary shudder ran through her.

"He'll be okay." Coda assured her. "We just have to smooth out the bump. You don't even need an eraser for that."

Fiona rubbed her palms together. "Should we call an ambulance?"

"No time, it's"—Coda looked up at the moon—"already nine o'clock. DaCapo will be back in twelve hours. That's one hour your time."

Fiona swallowed. Coda was right. "Okay, but we'll come back for him after we slow the metronome."

Coda finally saw Yip. He sat patiently beside her. His tail swished back and forth on the ground. She squealed with excitement and knelt to pet him. "Is it really you, Yip?"

He rubbed his head against her leg and jumped into her arms. "I missed you." He licked her cheek.

Coda giggled, "Mind if I borrow this?" she asked, reaching for the pencil.

Fiona nodded. It was both magical and terrifying to create things out of thin air. She didn't mind handing off the responsibility for a while. Coda drew a collar with a heart-shaped pendant around Yip's neck. In tiny letters she wrote, *If lost, return to Coda*.

"Cute," Ferris said, in a tone that implied he was over it. "Now can we take care of the guard? He can't just lie in the street."

Coda gave Yip a tight hug before picking up the guard by his feet. Fiona lifted him by the arms, and they carried him behind the bushes. There wasn't much Ferris or Yip could do to help, but the girls didn't need it. He weighed about as much as a paintbrush.

Coda surprised Fiona then. Instead of drawing rope to tie up the officer, she drew an eye mask and a pillow, which she tucked under his head. "There," she said. "Now you don't have to worry so much. He'll wake up confused but not angry."

Fiona was relieved. Coda was more bark than bite after all.

Ferris inspected the metronome's doors. "Locked," he said. "Can we draw a hole through them?"

Coda shook her head. "That will set off an alarm."

"A key?" suggested Fiona.

Coda shook her head again. "The doors open by facial recognition. We need someone to help get us in."

"What about the security guard?" asked Yip. "You could trace his face and hold up the drawing to the camera."

"Yes! That will work. What a good pet." Coda said, scratching Yip behind the ears.

Yip tried to conceal his pride, but his tail betrayed him as it wheeled around like a propeller.

Coda climbed behind the bushes to trace the security guard. She crouched down so she was no longer visible. Fiona's heartbeat quickened. What happens to the things hidden on a canvas? When you see a painting of mountains, there must be a sky beyond them, but does the sky exist if the artist hasn't painted it? Was Coda safe behind the bushes?

Her fear washed away as Coda reappeared holding a mask of the guard's face. It was flat and emotionless. The real guard looked peaceful as he slept, but the mask was lifeless. Yip's plan might not work. Surely, a facial recognition scanner would be able to tell the difference between a face and a drawing of one. Coda held the mask up to the scanner and Fiona held her breath.

A beam of light scanned the face. It was followed by a high-pitched beep and the sound of the doors unlocking. Fiona pulled open the doors to the giant metronome building. A wave of cool air blew her hood back onto her shoulders. She wouldn't need it now. She crossed the threshold into the dark, unembellished lobby.

Ferris leapt onto Fiona's shoulder as Coda ran to the elevator. Yip followed behind his creator admiringly. Fiona was suddenly all too aware of her heartbeat thumping in her ears. When she entered the elevator, Coda's steady breathing filled the small space. The silence of the building sank deep into her bones. The only place in Metronome no one could hear the ticking was inside the metronome itself.

"Which floor is it?" asked Fiona, her hand hovering over the panel of buttons. There were two hundred and one floors, one more than there had been in the last skyscraper.

Coda's mouth pulled to one side. "DaCapo doesn't let me anywhere near his office. This is the closest I've been."

"It'll be on the top floor," Ferris said.

"How do you know?" asked Yip.

"A man like that... someone seeking power. He'll put himself at the top so he can look down on everyone else," Ferris replied like he'd known DaCapo in another life.

Fiona pressed the button for the two hundred and first floor. Though they were unable to hear the metronome's ticks, the elevator zoomed upwards as fast as ever. The doors opened to a small room with a humble wooden desk and a carpeted floor.

"This is DaCapo's office?" asked Yip. He put his snoot to the carpet and sniffed around the room. "Smells too floral if you ask me." Then his nose came upon another facial recognition scanner.

"Shoot," said Coda. "How do we get past this one without a face to trace?"

Fiona's stomach dropped. They hadn't come all this way just to get stuck outside DaCapo's office. Had she set herself up to be caught by the shadow? She found herself backing away from the elevator. The shadow was just one of her problems. The mayor was another. What would he do when he found them? He'd have a cruel smile plastered on his face. His creased eyebrows would hover uncomfortably far over his eyelids. His tiny black eyes would bulge with anger. His—

Wait.

That was it. Fiona realized what she had to do. "I can draw the mayor," she said.

Ferris cocked his head. "Are you sure? That's a lot more complicated than a window."

"I'm sure." It wasn't like Fiona thought she was Leonardo DaVinci, but she didn't have to paint the Mona Lisa. She just had to draw a man with oversized eyebrows. "I can do it."

Coda handed Fiona the pencil.

Fiona closed her eyes and pictured DaCapo's smug face. Though she'd only just met him, with all that took place, it felt like she'd known him for weeks. She was adjusting to Metronome time. Funny how easily that happened.

She held the pencil in the air and outlined the mayor's stern face—his sunken black eyes, his rectangular nose, and his thick, spidery eyebrows. She drew his mouth a bit unevenly. It looked swollen on one side. But she had seen her mother's phone unlock even when her lipstick was smudgy, so the mask would pass facial recognition. Hopefully.

She held the mask in both hands and looked into the face of the man who wanted complete control. Now Fiona controlled him. She extended an arm and positioned the mask in front of the scanner.

Chapter 21

The scanner beeped, and the door to DaCapo's office opened with a hiss. The room held an imposing wingback leather chair behind an ornate, hand-crafted desk. A cigar vault lit up the far wall in greeting. Yip had been right. The room smelled of oak and camouflaged cigar smoke. Floor to ceiling windows revealed that this was the tallest point in Metronome. The tip of the metronome's pendulum ticked back and forth across the windows like windshield wipers. Portraits covered the wall. They were arranged in a pyramid with a name plate below each gaudy picture frame. Fiona felt like she was in some kind of art museum. The only thing that seemed out of place was a decades-old bulky computer that sat in the corner of DaCapo's desk.

A deep voice fell on Fiona's ears like syrup. "I don't remember getting here," it oozed.

Fiona froze. Yip arched his back in fear.

"What's going on with my mouth?" slurred the voice, becoming frantic. Ferris glanced around the room. When he couldn't find the source of the voice, he hopped under the mayor's desk.

"Where are my hands?" the voice bellowed. Coda ran behind the leather chair.

Though the voice sounded close, there was no movement in the room.

Then Fiona looked at the mask in her hands and the eyes of Mayor DaCapo blinked. She dropped the mask.

"*OUCHHH*," cried the mayor as his face landed flat against the floor.

Fiona looked at Ferris, fear in her eyes.

"Don't panic," Ferris said. "He's only a head."

Mayor DaCapo countered, "You should panic. I can still yell. *Help! Security! Police!*" he screamed.

Coda ran out from behind the chair and grabbed the mask. She put her hand over DaCapo's mouth. "If you don't be quiet, I'm going to throw you out the window!" she said.

FIONA AND THE FORGOTTEN PIANO

DaCapo bit Coda's hand and she yanked it away. "Fine, if that's how you want it..." Coda opened a drawer in the mayor's desk, threw the mask in and slammed the drawer shut.

DaCapo continued to yell, but his voice sounded far away now. Fiona held a hand to her heart to slow it down.

"Why is the mask alive?" asked Yip.

"I think..." Fiona gathered her thoughts. "I think when Coda traced the security guard, she captured the bump on his head, so the mask was sleeping just like he was. When I drew DaCapo, I drew him without any injuries. He came to life like everything else in this world."

"So we can draw a device to slow the metronome," Coda said excitedly.

Fiona shook her head. "I don't think so. The drawing still has to be accurate, and we don't know what a device like that would look like."

Coda nodded. "We search the room then. Keep an eye out for a lever or a dial."

Yip located the areas of the room where DaCapo spent the most time. Coda twisted the portraits at various angles, searching for hidden compartments. Fiona jumped around the office looking for squeaky floorboards that could hide a device, though it looked more like she was playing a game of hopscotch. It was Ferris who found something.

As he looked through the items on DaCapo's desk, he stepped on the computer's keyboard. The monitor lit up. The image was that of a ticking metronome, a smaller version of the one they were inside of. On the screen, the pendulum ticked fast, then slow, then fast again as a weight slid up and down the pendulum rod.

Ferris hopped around the keyboard pressing every button he could. "How do we control this thing?"

Fiona looked up from the floorboards and joined Ferris at the computer. "You need a password, but I don't know enough about the mayor to figure out what it would be."

Coda turned away from the portraits, seeming satisfied at the disarray she'd caused them. They now looked like a tower of wobbly blocks ready to topple. "My uncle has a lot of security. I don't think we'll be able to guess his password."

It was true. A building with facial recognition scanners at every door would have impenetrable passwords. Fiona watched the metronome on the screen. *Tick. Tick. Tick.* Maybe it was a touch screen. Ms. Downey had always been opposed to using a metronome in Fiona's piano lessons. "The timing should be in your head," she'd say. But Fiona still knew how to use one. The higher the weight on a metronome is, the slower it ticks. She positioned her finger on the screen over the metronome's weight and dragged it up.

A flashing red error alarmed.

Fingerprint not recognized. Enter password or try again.

Attempts Remaining: 2

Fiona's stomach squirmed with guilt. She'd wasted an attempt. Was it possible they could break into DaCapo's computer with only two more guesses? "There is no way I can draw the mayor's fingerprint," she muttered.

"Let's look for a note," said Coda who was trying to be helpful but seemed to be running out of ideas. "Maybe DaCapo keeps his password on a post-it."

"Let's ask the mask," Ferris suggested.

Yip opened the desk drawer with his teeth.

The mask of DaCapo gasped. "Finally, fresh air," he breathed. It was quite dramatic for someone who'd been in the drawer such a short time.

"What's the password for the computer?" Ferris interrogated from atop the desk.

"How should I know? I've only been the mayor a few minutes," the mask retorted.

"Where's the dark cell?" demanded Fiona. It felt strange to demand something from someone, even if that someone was a two-dimensional head.

"Same answer. How should I know?"

Coda slammed the drawer shut in frustration.

The mask's voice echoed from inside the closed drawer. "Would a big red button help?"

Coda opened the drawer forcefully. The mask slid to the front of it. "What are you talking about?" she asked.

"There's a big red button in here, right at the top of the drawer."

"Ferris, hop in there and see if he's lying," said Coda.

"A please would be nice," said Ferris as he dropped down into the drawer. He landed with one foot on the DaCapo double's forehead. The mask stuck to his foot. He shook it off like it was a stray piece of toilet paper. He looked up. "That's a big red button alright."

"Push it," said Coda. Fiona thought Coda might be pushing her luck with Ferris's patience.

"We don't know what it does," the frog protested.

"What's the worst that happens? We blow up?" Yip teased.

Ferris grunted and pressed the button.

A whoosh of air escaped like a sigh from the cigar vault on the far wall. Fiona examined it. Scents of cedar and smoke overwhelmed her airways. She coughed. The vault was no longer pressed against the wall but jutted out at an angle, leaving a slight opening. She pressed the edge of her palms into the open space and pushed the vault further. It opened on well-oiled hinges. Behind it was a dark room. A very dark room. A room so black Fiona couldn't tell if there was anything there at all. It made her woozy. It felt like the darkness was pulling her in. She put a hand on the wall to steady herself.

"Nori?" she whispered. It felt wrong to speak into the darkness at full volume.

"*Cree cree!*" Nori exclaimed, appearing from the dark and jumping into Fiona's arms with a thump.

"I'm so sorry I got you locked in there." She cradled Nori in the nook of her elbow. Nori's heart pulsed against her forearm, whether out of fear or relief, Fiona couldn't tell. "I'm learning to pick my battles. A power-hungry mayor wasn't a great place to start. It won't happen again."

Nori smiled sweetly up at Fiona and nuzzled her arm in forgiveness. Fiona ran a finger down the axolotl's back. It had a chill to it. The dark was a cold place. But Nori didn't shiver. She was okay. The guilt Fiona had been holding onto began to evaporate. She placed Nori on the desk next to Ferris.

"You doing okay?" Ferris asked.

Nori stood tall and fluttered her gills. A little darkness couldn't hurt her.

Yip was eager to meet the new creature. He lifted his front paws onto the desk where she stood and sniffed. Nori sniffed him right back. Though relief settled in the room, the metronome on the computer monitor continued to tick maddeningly. How long had this computer controlled the giant metronome? Was it older than Fiona was? Was it older than the mayor himself? An idea popped into her head. Even though the computer was old, it probably still had internet access. Fiona decided to take a chance. Into the password box, she typed: *Torien, we need your help.*

Incorrect Password. Try again.

Attempts Remaining: 1

The flashing red error alarmed.

"What did you do?" Coda asked.

"I asked for help," Fiona said, her voice weak. Her cheeks burned, suddenly unsure about what she'd done. She hoped it had been the right decision. Time was running out and the mayor—the real one—would be returning to work any minute now. With every second that passed, Fiona worried she'd wasted an attempt.

"Who did you—" Coda stopped mid-sentence as the screen turned a bright blue and the face of Torien Umba appeared.

"Such a tiny screen," Torien complained. But after a moment, he seemed to settle in, as he realized a small screen meant his head couldn't drift away. "I see you haven't made it to Fugue yet," he said bluntly.

Fiona shook her head. "We tried. Arti gave us a key to Chords. The card readers there sent us to a yellow geyser. We found the geyser, but I mixed up the keys and then we couldn't leave Metronome because we were in jail, and they had our friend and... it's been a lot."

Torien frowned. "I told you your key would be near the Great Piano, so I'm not sure why you went to all those other places."

"You didn't tell us that," Fiona corrected gently. "You never finished your sentence. The internet cut out."

Caught off guard, Torien backed away from the screen. His head became the size of a lollipop. "Oh... I hadn't noticed that." It seemed there was a flaw in Torien's technology. When the internet had cut out, so had his consciousness. He didn't know he hadn't finished his conversation with Fiona. "What I meant to say was that you'll find the key on its way to a nearby piano. When you get lost, you seek something familiar. Keys are the same way. If the key to Fugue couldn't find its way back to the Great Piano, it would have chosen the next best thing."

Ferris blinked and turned to Fiona. They seemed to be having the same thought at the same time. Was it possible? After everything they'd been through together, could the key really be where their journey had started?

Fiona's piano, the one she practiced scales on every Friday evening, was quite close to the Great Piano. In fact, it was only a few hundred yards away. The key to Fugue could have made its way there.

Ferris spoke the words they were both thinking. "We have to get home—to your house, I mean."

Chapter 22

Yip barked. "DaCapo is coming! I can smell him."

Fiona tossed Coda the pencil. "Quick, lock the door."

Coda ran to it. She drew every kind of lock there was. Then she drew them all again. Two chain locks, two padlocks, and two deadbolts held the door closed. They weren't the neatest of locks, but they'd do the trick.

Fiona and Yip pushed the leather chair across the floor to block the entrance. Ferris peered at the street two hundred one stories below them. They wouldn't survive a jump from that height. They could draw a hot air balloon if it came to that.

Nori seemed oblivious to the state of panic in the room. Perhaps her time in the dark cell had given her a different perspective on things. While the others were blocking DaCapo's entry and planning their escape, Nori was making friends with the screen-bound Torien. He seemed to have no trouble understanding her squeaks.

"*Coqui*," said Nori pointing to Coda.

"I knew a Coda once," said Torien. "Did you know it means—"

"Who is that?" Fiona asked, pointing to one of the portraits on the wall. Her finger shook slightly. The face she saw was flat and sunken in. The eyes had been drawn closed. But still, it was a face she knew.

Coda shrugged. "That's the Head of Security. Why?"

Fiona stepped into the seat of the leather chair, then balanced on its arm. She read the name under the portrait. Anita Downey. *Ms. Downey*. Fiona's piano teacher was DaCapo's Head of Security.

Fiona felt as though she'd stepped in a patch of quicksand, like she was being pulled downwards as she tried to connect the dots. Had Ms. Downey been protecting DaCapo this whole time? Was that the reason she'd only learned scales? Was it some twisted way of keeping Fiona away from the piano? Was Ms. Downey watching everyone that lived outside the Fermata woods?

She had so many questions. And yet, the one question she'd been asking herself since entering the woods had been answered. Ms. Downey was the shadow. She could sense it somehow. The shadow had the same dreary presence as her teacher, the kind that put everyone around her in a sour mood. But it wasn't just how the shadow made her feel. It looked the same too. The shadow's figure was narrow with straight hair. It was the same height as her teacher. It had no hands—or at least it looked like it didn't have hands. Fiona was reminded of the way Ms. Downey's stretched-out sweater always fell past her fingertips. Now she knew why Ms. Downey was always drained and colorless. She didn't belong in Fiona's world. She belonged in Metronome.

A bang on the door interrupted Fiona's racing thoughts.

"It's him," squeaked Yip, ears pointed straight up. His tail was rigid with nerves.

The mayor shouted through the door. "We have you on video breaking an entering and taking out a security guard. Open the door before I sentence you to eternity in the dark cell."

Fiona wasn't going to let that happen. She opened the top drawer in DaCapo's desk and grabbed the mask. She whispered something in its ear and held it towards the office door.

The mask bellowed, "Who are you and why are you pretending to be the mayor?"

On the other side of the door, the mayor was stunned into silence.

The mask continued. "I've called security, and they will be escorting you out of this building immediately."

"*Excuse me*," Mayor DaCapo roared. "I don't know what you've got going on in there, but there is no way out. Have fun spending the next ten years in the dark cell." It sounded as if DaCapo was going to knock down the door with his fists. He shouted again. This time it was muffled, like he was speaking to someone else. "Get me a pencil and my security fleet immediately."

Fiona began to draw furiously. She had done a pretty good job of drawing the mayor's face. If she could draw DaCapo's body, she could attach it to the mask and make an entirely new mayor. She drew DaCapo's eight sides and dressed them in the suit he'd been wearing when they'd met. It wasn't her best work, but it should trick a bunch of fast-acting security guards. She crossed her fingers just in case.

Fiona attached the mask to DaCapo's body. The DaCapo double rolled his neck. He stretched his arms above his head. "Feels good to be whole." He took in a deep breath and put his hands to his stomach like he was discovering it for the first time, which, of course, he was. "What can I do to help?"

"The mayor and his guards are going to break through those locks any second now," said Fiona. "You need to distract them long enough so we can get out of here and back to the tree portal."

The DaCapo double grinned. "I'll do more than that." He took a few steps towards the window. "I think I'd like to be mayor." The double stood with such confidence Fiona imagined crowds cheering his name at his next political speech. "Anyway, this other guy sounds boorish if you ask me. But yes, for now, I'll help you get to the portal."

Torien called out from the computer. "Fiona, I have something you might want to hear—Coda too."

Fiona hesitated, afraid to turn her back to the door. There were already cracks forming at the edges. The guards were drawing their way in. But she had called Torien for a reason. Maybe he knew something that would help.

"In music," Torien said, "Coda is a passage that brings a piece to an end. Because your friend shares her name with this musical element, she has the ability to bring your journey to an end. She can draw a door that will take you home."

Before Fiona could process what Torien had said, a guard kicked in the office door. The winged-back chair did nothing to stop him entering. It fell over like it was playing dead. The mayor entered the room backed by six polygonal guards. "Arrest them," he declared.

Fiona, Coda, and Yip backed into the corner of the room. Ferris and Nori were nowhere to be seen. Hopefully, they were hiding somewhere safe.

The DaCapo double stepped in front of Fiona. "No! Arrest this imposter!" He shouted pointing at the mayor.

The security guards looked between the two DaCapos. Fiona held her breath. The DaCapo double's suit was not quite as sharp as the real one's. There were white spaces in it where the shading wasn't all the way filled in. If only she had time to fix it.

"Preposterous!" shouted the mayor.

"Indeed!" shouted the double. "How many fingers does the real mayor have?"

The question caught even Fiona off guard. A mixture of annoyance and confusion crossed the mayor's face. "What kind of question is that?" he snarled. "I have ten fingers."

"No," replied the double. "*I* have ten fingers." He held up his hands and wiggled his fingers for the guards to see. "You sir, have eight fingers... and one ear I might add."

"What nonsense is this? I have always had ten fingers. Here is the pr—" The mayor trailed off as he held his hands up. He was missing his thumb on one hand and his pinky on the other. He quickly reached to his ears and found the right one was gone.

Fiona saw a flash of orange as Ferris jumped off of the mayor's shoulder. She saw another as Nori climbed down his pant leg. They scurried under the desk. Ferris looked at Fiona and winked.

The security guards mumbled in unison, "I'm sorry, Mayor. My apologies, Mayor. Never doubting you again, sir."

The guards handcuffed a fuming DaCapo. There was practically smoke coming out of his ears. If the mayor's face could've turned red from anger, Fiona was sure his would be a deep scarlet. "I'm coming for you, Coda," he hissed. "You'll see. I'll lock Yip away again. I'll sentence your friends to life in the dark cell. Metronome will be nothing without me."

The guards dragged DaCapo back. But then, in unison, they stopped. The largest one held his hand to his ear. "She says to wait."

Fiona pushed her shoulders back unconsciously. She didn't have to ask who the "she" was the guards were referring to. The elevator outside DaCapo's office dinged and in walked Ms. Downey. She looked different. Less drained. More human, if that was possible. It was like the metronome's speed had the opposite effect on her as it did the rest of the citizens. Where they might fall apart as the ticking sped up, Ms. Downey thrived in the speed of it. It was scary.

Fiona felt like shrinking. Her worlds were colliding. At home, she was hesitant, shy, obedient. But in the worlds connected by the Great Piano, she had learned she could be more than that. In Metronome, she was decisive, quick-witted, and brave. She wanted to hold on to that part of her. But seeing Ms. Downey now—the teacher who never thought she was good enough, the one who never let her grow—she froze.

"Idiots," Ms. Downey reprimanded. "You do know how these lot escaped jail, don't you? They erased the bars. Why would you think they couldn't erase a finger or an ear just as easily?"

The guards mumbled their apologies.

"That's why you're in charge."

"Didn't think of that."

"Has anyone got an eraser?"

They checked their pockets but came up empty. For now, DaCapo remained in handcuffs. "Imbeciles," he muttered.

"And you," Ms. Downey locked eyes with Fiona. "Why couldn't you just stay home?" Her eyes darted to Ferris. "It's his fault isn't it? You wouldn't leave on your own."

"You'd be surprised," Ferris said.

Ms. Downey rolled her eyes. "I never meant to open that door. The one to Fugue. Didn't expect anyone would come out of it though. You frogs are almost as closed off as Metronome. I would've taken over that world too if—"

"Taken over?" DaCapo asked gruffly. "I'm in charge here. You're merely my number two."

"Is that so?" Ms. Downey asked. "You still haven't figured out how to leave this place. As far as we know, I'm the only person who can leave Metronome and still keep my form. It seems like that would make me in charge, don't you think?"

DaCapo made a sound that was somewhere between a snarl and a grunt.

Ms. Downey rolled her eyes. "Get him out of here," she instructed the guards. "Any cell will do. We don't want him thinking he's special." The guards exited the mayor's office, dragging a squirming DaCapo along.

Ms. Downey turned back to Fiona, a look of pity on her face. "And I went through all the trouble of procuring a Sound Bubble, so you'd never hear the woods again."

"You did what?" Torien spoke up.

"You're here too? What is this? Some kind of reunion?" Ms. Downey seemed startled seeing Torien's face on DaCapo's computer screen, but she quickly recovered. "Well, there's no sense pretending now. Yes, I stole your technology. Disguised myself as that lawyer of yours. It wasn't hard. You Electronicans are always playing with your appearances." Ms. Downey stepped closer to Fiona. "Now, what do you say to spending some time in the dark cell?"

Fiona backed away.

Ms. Downey stepped closer still. "Oh, come now. It won't be so bad. All of your insignificant friends will be in there with you."

"They're not insignificant," Fiona finally spoke up. "You might be able to travel through worlds, but you're still made of charcoal like the rest of them. I can still erase you."

"Oh, but you wouldn't." Ms. Downey's voice was sickly sweet. "You couldn't live with yourself if you did that."

Fiona remained stone faced. Though Ms. Downey was right. Fiona couldn't erase someone. She couldn't take away their existence. But she couldn't let Ms. Downey know that. And she had to keep her teacher's attention, because behind her, Coda was drawing a trap.

Chapter 23

"You don't know what I'd do," Fiona said, spitting into her palm.

It was a bluff. Fiona was so thirsty she barely had any saliva left, but she only had to distract Ms. Downey a bit longer. She took a step forward, and to her surprise, Ms. Downey took a step back. Her bluff was working.

"Whatever you do to me, I can draw it right back," Ms. Downey said, suddenly unable to look Fiona in the eyes. Her confidence was faltering as Fiona's grew.

"I'm sure you could," Fiona said, inching closer.

Ms. Downey used DaCapo's desk to put space between her and Fiona. It was exactly where they needed her. "I have pencils hidden all over this room, you know."

"And you think the guards would help you? After how you've treated them?" Fiona asked.

"I'm certain they would."

"How certain?" Fiona leaned over the desk and swiped a hand toward Ms. Downey. Ms. Downey tripped over her heels and fell into the armchair.

She kept falling then, through the hole Coda had drawn in the seat. A hole that led much farther down than anyone could see. Ms. Downey disappeared from view without so much as a yelp.

"Where'd she go?" Fiona asked.

"I sent her somewhere she can't hurt anyone," Coda said.

"Which world did you pick?" Torien asked.

"I think it's called Cantata," Coda said.

"Good choice. I'd like to watch her try and control mermaids."

"I'd like to see her try to swim," Coda chuckled.

"Well done, everyone," said the DaCapo double with a clap. His tone made it sound as though they'd hit a fundraising goal not sent Ms. Downey to another world. "All in a day's work, I suppose." The double dusted off his hands and made his way behind the mayor's desk as if there had never been another DaCapo. He pulled out the armchair to sit and then thought better of it. Coda threw Yip the pencil. He caught it in his mouth and scribbled over the hole in the armchair. DaCapo continued, "I imagine you three want to get home now."

Ferris threw his head back. "Yes, finally," he rasped.

"Is there anything I can do for you before you go?"

Fiona hesitated. For the first time in a long time, she had just about everything she wanted. Nori was free. Ferris was almost home, for real this time. They'd thwarted the mayor and her piano teacher. There wasn't much more she could ask for. Then the ticking of the metronome jogged her memory. "You could slow the metronome," she said.

Coda agreed. "It doesn't have to be super slow, just slow enough that people can walk for a change. Maybe even take a leisurely stroll."

The mayor sat in his chair. He put his feet up on the desk and his hands behind his head. "Yes. I could," he said satisfactorily.

"That sounds like my cue to leave," said Torien, who didn't seem to appreciate DaCapo's feet in his face. "It was... not terrible getting to meet you all. Best wishes, Nori."

"*Peeep.*" Nori hopped, and the screen returned to the image of the ticking metronome.

The mayor placed his fingers on the keyboard and typed the password. "Ah, muscle memory," he said. He leaned forward in his chair and touched the screen, sliding the weight on the metronome up. The pendulum outside slowed.

Fiona looked out over the city and saw the sun pause. The cars braked. The people stopped running. She could feel the world exhaling as it slowed down.

"Thank you, DaCapo," she said with a smile. "I'm glad I drew you."

♪♫♩♬♪♪♫

Coda stood with the pencil in hand. She lifted her arm, then dropped it. She didn't know how to draw a passage to bring Fiona home. After all, she'd only just learned she had the ability to do it. "It can't be just any old door," she said quietly.

"You drew the trap for Anita. You can do this. Trust your instincts," Ferris advised.

Coda nodded and stood straighter. She held the pencil high in the air and drew an oval large enough for Fiona to pass through. Then she drew a large cross through the center of it.

The shapes glimmered before transforming into a three-dimensional door. Compared to Fiona's hand-drawn elevator, the door was impressive. It looked sturdy, like it might be difficult to open. Was it because the door was made to connect worlds? Or was it because Coda had drawn it? The charcoal girl gripped the edge of the cross, which was now a shining silver handle and pulled. Or maybe yanked is a better word for it. The door was indeed as solid as it looked.

With a final tug, the door slid open. Light and color tiptoed into the room. On the other side of the door was a piano. Not the Great Piano from the forest, but the regular piano from Fiona's living room. Fiona squeezed Coda's hand. "You can come with us if you want."

Coda smiled halfheartedly. "Thanks for the offer," she shrugged.

Fiona heard the words Coda couldn't say. Fiona's world, the one with bright yellow sun and the damp rainy days, wasn't made for girls like Coda. A girl made of charcoal couldn't survive the real world. Ms. Downey was the only person who'd ever figured out how to do it. And she wasn't exactly the kind of person one should ask for advice. Nor was she in a place to give it.

"Yip and I have some catching up to do anyway. Plus, I have to get to know my new uncle."

"I'll need an Assistant Mayor," DaCapo chimed in.

Coda shed Fiona's jacket from her shoulders. "You should take this though."

Fiona shook her head. "Why don't you keep it? With your uncle gone, maybe you can have some color."

Coda squealed and hugged the coat to her chest. "I'll cherish it." Her eyes gleamed. "Watch out, Metronome, the Assistant Mayor is here!"

Fiona laughed. "Now that you have your own superpower, you can draw a passage to visit anytime you want."

Yip nudged Fiona's hand with his nose as a casual reminder he was still there.

Fiona stroked his head. "You're welcome to visit too, Yip."

Ferris and Nori said goodbye, each in their own way. Ferris gave a simple nod. Nori nuzzled Coda's feet almost as lovingly as Yip would. Fiona scooped up the amphibians and placed them on her shoulders, Ferris on her left and Nori on her right. Her mouth flattened into a line then, taking another moment to consider her surroundings. It felt strange to be going home. As much as Metronome was a strange place, she had learned a lot here. She hoped she could carry it with her. What if she forgot everything as soon as she passed through the door?

The weight of Ferris and Nori on her shoulders reminded her she didn't have a choice. She had to get home as much as they did. "Thanks for the adventure," she said. Then she stepped through the door.

It took a moment for Fiona to realize it should not have been light out. Every other time they'd returned to the woods, it had still been dark. No time had passed. Had Coda's passage brought them through time?

Fiona remembered what Arti said: "As long as you don't stay for more than a week, you'll return at the same time you left." With how time passed in Metronome, could it have been a week already?

The microwave clock said it was seven. And not that she was an astronomer, but based on the sun's position, Fiona guessed it was morning. Her parents would normally be awake by now. She stepped further into the living room. What about the door? If her parents were awake, what would they think seeing Fiona appear from a drawn portal? She whipped around but the door was gone.

Still no sign of Fiona's parents, she deduced it must be Sunday, the only day of the week they didn't wake her up with banging pots and loud whispers. She exhaled a relieving breath. At least she hadn't missed much. Maybe her parents would sleep in long enough that Fiona could visit Fugue. It would be nice to experience some fog after the dry charcoal city. It would be nice to have a glass of water too.

Ferris hopped on top of the piano where the vase of daffodils sat from the day before. A plume of yellow pollen fell from the flowers. It looked a bit like a geyser. Ferris shook the golden flakes off his back. He peered over the edge of the piano and whispered, "Which one do you think it is?"

Fiona looked at the keys and knew. It was the sticking black key from her piano lesson. That's why it didn't fit in the piano. It belonged to a different one. How had Ms. Downey not caught that?

Fiona sat at the piano bench and gave the key a gentle pull. It slid out from the keybed like a stick of softened butter. She had no pockets to put the key in, but she didn't want to let it out of her sight anyway.

The trio walked through the forest; sunlight peppered the leaves. Fiona knew the way to the Great Piano well now. Her heart fluttered. She couldn't wait to see Ferris's home. She decided that even if her parents did wake up and she got in trouble, this was more important.

Fiona placed the key in the piano bed. A sense of calm ran through her. She knew it was the right key this time. Ferris and Nori hopped in to attach it. The resulting note was deep and comforting.

"That's the one," Ferris said. He jumped into Fiona's cupped hands. "I can feel the fog already." He wriggled his body like he'd just put on the coziest silk pajamas.

Nori took off, the fastest of the three. Fiona expected Ferris to follow, but he stayed cradled in the curves of her palm. One last ride before home, she supposed. Nori was already a bouncing orange ball in the trees ahead, so Fiona used the note to guide her. She didn't trip once.

The sound ended at a juniper bush. Fiona touched the needle-like leaves. "It's not really a tree," she said. The bush was full and thick, but it was about a foot shorter than she was. And she was nowhere near as tall as most trees.

"*Wheeek*," said Nori excitedly. She scurried around the bush. At her small size, it was plenty big enough to be a tree.

"Where's the entrance?" asked Fiona.

Ferris inspected the bush. He crawled under the branches and when he reappeared, his mood changed. "We're in the right place, but the door..." Ferris didn't meet Fiona's gaze. "It's only big enough for frogs."

Fiona deflated. "Oh." Her heart fell into her stomach. She crossed her legs and sat on the ground. She didn't care about the dirt or the morning dew. Her pajamas had experienced worse. "I can't visit."

Ferris shook his head. "I'm sorry." He put his hand on her foot.

Nori climbed into Fiona's lap and looked at her with puppy dog eyes. "*Pio coqui peep*," she said.

"No, it's okay." Fiona stroked Nori's back. Just as Fiona was starting to understand Nori, she had to let her go. "You go with Ferris. You'll be happy in Fugue."

Nori climbed up Fiona's arm and pushed her head into Fiona's shoulder. A warm tear rolled down Fiona's cheek. She brushed it away.

"We'll come back to visit you," Ferris reassured her. "We can have a messaging system. Leave an acorn by the portal when you want visitors."

"You're always welcome," Fiona laughed through another tear.

"Be back tomorrow then." The side of Ferris's mouth curled up, the sarcastic frog replaced by a caring one.

Fiona didn't believe him, but it was nice to hear.

"I'll bring Louis."

"I'd like that," Fiona said. She picked Ferris up and held him to her for a hug. And though the frog wasn't the hugging type, he leaned in too. "Now go soak up some fog," she said, setting him down.

Ferris nodded. He held onto Fiona's finger for a second longer, then he and Nori disappeared under the bush.

Fiona sat for a moment alone. Her lip quivered. She bit it to stop it from shaking. She hadn't lost her friends. They were just going home.

Fiona untied her left shoe. She pulled the shoelace out from her sneaker and draped it around the top of the bush. She tied a bow around the top branch. If anything happened to the piano or its keys, she could find her way back to Fugue, and she could leave an acorn for Ferris so he knew to visit.

Fiona entered the back door to her home, planning to sneak into her room and get under the covers as if she'd been asleep all night. She could use a nap anyway. But when she passed by the piano, now missing a key, she headed for the shared phone. It was charging on the end table. She typed "piano technician" into the search bar and called the first number on the list. She didn't expect a technician would answer this early, but could she leave a voicemail. She wasn't sure if she'd have piano lessons anytime soon, but she would practice on her own. She had to at least learn a real song. Did she still remember how to play Minuet in D Minor? She wasn't sure she'd ever really known how. Her recital seemed like it was ages ago.

Fiona hung up the phone and plugged it back in. She tried not to make the living room floorboards creak as she walked back into the kitchen. She glanced up from the floor. Her mother was at the stove quietly making pancakes. Fiona jumped. How long had her mom been there?

"How were they?" her mother asked, still facing the stovetop.

Fiona paused. Was her mom asking about the well-being of the piano technician? "How were who?"

"My sisters, your aunts, Rina and Mari."

Fiona turned an ear towards her mother, not quite sure she'd heard her correctly. "My—your—they were—You're Vihuela?" she stammered.

Her mom flipped a pancake without missing a beat. "What did you think V. was short for?"

Fiona inched her shoulders upwards. "Victoria, I guess."

Her mother laughed, "I never did correct Anita when she called me that. Well, now you know. I'm a card reader."

Fiona sat at the counter, suddenly awake. There was a reason she had felt at peace in the triplets' tent. They were family. Chords was her second home. "But your hair isn't blue like Rina and Mari said."

"Not at the moment. Blue isn't a very common hair color for moms. I dyed it so no one would be suspicious." Fiona's mother sprinkled chocolate chips over the pancake. "My sisters told you that though, in their closing show. *Waves like the ocean, now midnight black. We can't wait to have our family back.*"

Fiona popped a chocolate chip in her mouth. "I only heard the part about waves like the ocean. I thought they were warning us about the frozen sea in Minor Chords."

Her mom nodded, sliding a plate over to Fiona.

"How come we never visited?"

"You've seen how hard it is to travel through the worlds," her mother admitted. "People steal keys. They hide them, hoard them. I miss my sisters, but the timing was never right."

Fiona had to agree. She'd traveled through four worlds just to get Ferris home. "Why did you leave in the first place?"

"Your father grew up in this house. I met him in the woods on my way to Sonata. He had an axe. He was going to cut down a tree for firewood. I stopped him, of course, because what he was about to cut down was a tree portal." Fiona's mother grabbed maple syrup from the fridge. "I didn't travel for weeks after that. I was nervous I'd go into a portal, and I wouldn't be able to come back out. I asked the cards how I could protect the worlds within the trees. They showed me this house, a place I could live while I watched over the woods. But more importantly, they showed me a future with the man I'd met and our brave daughter. I couldn't stay in Chords when I knew you were meant to grow up here. Those freckles of yours, they show your talent just as my hair shows mine. Only, they're much more rare than blue or green hair. You're a protector, Fiona. It's why you felt the need to lead Ferris home. It's why you saved Nori. It's why you never told me how the kids at school had treated you. You were even protecting me. I hope you know now it's important to protect yourself too."

Fiona nodded.

Her mother slid a perfectly fluffy pancake onto a plate. "It's also why I believe you are destined to be the next Protector of the Keys. You're meant to keep the worlds of the Great Piano open." She poured the syrup over her pancakes and looked at Fiona in a way she hadn't before. Instead of motherly concern, Fiona saw trust in her eyes. "Do you think you can do that?"

Protector of the Keys. Fiona let the words sink in. They felt right. They explained her sudden musical abilities and how she knew where each key in the piano was supposed to go. And she did want to protect the worlds. They needed to be open. In just one week, Fiona had learned it wasn't rude to ask questions or say no. She learned people would listen to her when she spoke, and she learned to stand up for her friends. Most of all, she learned her freckles weren't something to hide. They were beautiful and meaningful and part of who she was. Seeing the trust in her mother's eyes, Fiona felt she could take on anything. She smiled. "Let's see what the cards say."

Acknowledgements

Like the Great Piano, the people who shaped this book cannot be forgotten.

Thank you to the Wild Ink family— editor Laura Wackwitz for believing in my story and making it shine, cover designer Olivia Hunter for bringing Fiona to life, and publisher Abigail Wild for giving Fiona a home.

To my critique partners, Patchree and Rennae whose guidance, encouragement and feedback transformed Fiona and her journey.

Thank you to my supportive family and friends. I'm lucky to say there are a lot of you. To my mom, who read every version of this story and my dad, for reading this book even though fantasy isn't really your genre. To

Paxton, who pushed me to keep querying. Right now, you are more into eating books than reading them, but I'm sure that will change someday. Thank you, Liz, Suzanne, Ken, and Ali. Your encouragement and enthusiasm for me and my story mean so much. Finally, to Manny, for not batting an eye as I reenacted Arti standing on his head in our kitchen; thank you for always believing I could be a published author.

About Kate DeMaio

Kate grew up in Salem, Massachusetts, surrounded by ghost stories and witch tales. As a microbiologist, she studies the tiny worlds of bacteria, viruses and antibodies. As a writer, she creates magical worlds of her own. Kate now lives just outside of Boston with her husband, son, dog and cat.